Cricket

A Tale Of Humble Life

by

SILAS K. HOCKING
AUTHOR OF 'HER BENNY' AND 'CHIPS'

BOOK CLEARANCE CENTRE
27-28 DAWSON WAY, ST. JOHN'S SHOPPING PRECINCT,
LIVERPOOL, L1 1LH.

Published by:
Northern Publishing Services
28 Bedford Road
Firswood M16 0JA
Tel: **0161 862 9399**

THIS EDITION OF "CRICKET"
was first published in 1886

ISBN 1 899181 14 8

Reprint organised by:

Cliff Hayes

Printed & bound by:
Manchester Free Press
Tel: **0161 864 4540**

Frontispiece.   Cricket and her Mother in the Garden.

CRICKET

A TALE OF HUMBLE LIFE.

BY

SILAS K. HOCKING

Author of "Her Benny," "Sea Waif," etc., etc., etc.

" I'll carry you as far as I can."

LONDON
FREDERICK WARNE AND CO
AND NEW YORK.

Silas Kitto Hocking was born on the 24th March 1850 in the village of St. Stephens, Cornwall. The son of a Cornish mine owner he had a protected, middle class, Christian upbringing. Early in life he decided that he was interested in The Church and at the age of 17 was invited to address his local Non-Conformist Chapel.

After two small preaching posts around the country he was over-awed when offered a chance to join the prestigious circuit in Liverpool. Being a stranger to the city he was offered accommodation by the circuit steward Mr Richard Lloyd which he accepted, little knowing that three years later he would marry the daughter. As the youngest preacher he was given the poorest area, the down-town church and two small ones across the water at Birkenhead and Seacombe to look after. It was this post which led him to meeting the waifs and strays of Liverpool's streets that form so much of this book, and his travelling across on the Ferry became part of the story line. He spent three years in Liverpool and wrote about the joy he got from helping the down and out and the relaxation and pleasure of attending the organ recitals in St. George's Hall on his days off. He moved to the circuit in Manchester and spent two years there.

Circuit work was not entirely to his liking, and when he was offered his own church in Burnley he took up the offer. It was there he took up writing as a relaxation. The manuscript was called "Alec Green" and when it was almost finished he showed it to a friend over dinner who happened to be the editor of the Burnley Advertiser, who persuaded him to let it be published (anonymously Hocking insisted) in the Burnley Advertiser. It caught the public's imagination, and Hocking cut out the columns and sent them to F.Warne & Co. asking if they would be interested in the book. Warne agreed and sent him a cheque for £15 for copyright to the book.

One afternoon he was called upon to present the Sunday School Prizes, and browsed through the book that they had decided to give that year as the Prize. Quite incensed by the descriptions in the book of all the street urchins being no-goods and thieves beyond redemption, and implying that they were there because of their own misdeeds, he rushed home and started putting down on paper what he considered was a truer picture of how these children ended up in their sorry plight. "There but for God could be each one of us" was his theme, and that night "Her Benny" was born. He persuaded the Editor of his church's magazine 'The Denominational' to reluctantly carry the story as a serial, they were worried that it would upset some of their older readers - it didn't, and was an immediate success and lifted the magazine's circulation and standing.

He moved to a church in Manchester, and fell in with J. Marshall Mather of the Manchester City Mission, who he met in the Friends Meeting House in Mount Street. He accompanied his friend on his trips feeding the poor, and found out the workings of the soup kitchens and night shelters, that the Manchester City Mission had set up.

"Manchester did not suit my health" said Hocking and after three years there he took up a post in 1883 at Southport and the challenge of the new chapel in Duke Street which had just been built to replace the old one on Lord Street. The Chapel was hopelessly in debt with only a small congregation, but he threw himself into the post and within 12 months the chapel had nearly 1,000 people every Sunday and were almost out of debt.

In 1895 he retired to concentrate on writing which by now was earning money for his charities. In 1923 he wrote his biography; a very rare book, it is called "My Book of Memories". Silas passed away on 15th September 1935 in Hornsey, Highgate, North London.

CLIFF HAYES

"Am I so changed that you do not know me?"—p. 235

ⳫⳫⳫⳫⳫⳫⳫⳫⳫⳫⳫⳫⳫⳫⳫⳫⳫⳫⳫⳫⳫⳫⳫⳫⳫⳫⳫⳫⳫⳫ

What the critics said about the book when it first appeared.

"Its is an excellent story, capitally told."

THE TIMES

"It is a pretty and touching story."

SPECTATOR

"Since the days of 'Her Benny' Mr Hocking has done nothing better than 'Cricket.'"

MANCHESTER EXAMINER

ⳎⳎⳎⳎⳎⳎⳎⳎⳎⳎⳎⳎⳎⳎⳎⳎⳎⳎⳎⳎⳎⳎⳎⳎⳎⳎⳎⳎⳎⳎⳎⳎ

CONTENTS

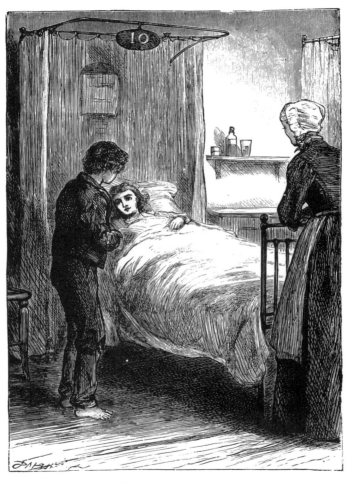

"I am so glad you're come."—p. 150

CRICKET.

CHAPTER I.

"I LOVE THE MOUNTAINS SO."

> " Their rocky summits, split and rent,
>   Formed turret, dome, and battlement,
>   Or seemed fantastically set
>   With cupola or minaret ;
>   Wild crests as pagod ever decked,
>   Or mosque of Eastern architect. "
>
> Scott.

THE house was low and long, with a thatched roof and whitewashed walls. In front was a long strip of garden, with a gravelled path that led down to a wooden gate, painted green, which opened out into a country lane, narrow and tortuous, winding in and out between quick-set hedges, but apparently leading nowhere in particular. On one side the garden was separated from the adjoining fields by a little stream of water, perfectly clear, which had fretted for itself a channel about two feet deep, and night and day rippled on with pleasant dreamy music, and never tired of its ceaseless song. On the same side, beyond the stretch of fields, rose hilly and broken country, well wooded, and swept at present with summer's living green ; and beyond this again the glorious Welsh mountains loomed up, solemn and grand.

On the other side of the garden, through vistas of elm and sycamore, stretched away level fields of pasture-land and ripening corn as far as eye could reach, all aglow at this moment with the golden rays of the sinking sun. At the end of the house grew a tall sycamore, and not two yards from the door was a giant hawthorn tree, with a rustic bench carried round its gnarled and knotted trunk.

On this bench sat a pale, sweet-faced woman, engaged on some article of infant's attire, but every now and then lifting her eyes to the far-off mountains that were beginning to burn in the

ruddy light of the setting sun. Martha Chase
never tired of these glorious mountains. Her early
home lay beyond them, miles and miles away.
More years than she cared to count had passed
since she visited the old spot, and only at very rare
intervals did she hear from home. Her father and
mother were both living, but were too old to under-
take the long journey, for they lived many miles
from any railway, and Martha herself was always
too full-handed to spare the time to visit them.

It is true that every winter she promised herself
that when summer came she would visit her parents
at Cefn-Lee, but when summer came something or
other was sure to block the way, and so the seasons
came and went, and the visit was never paid.

But the longing remained, nevertheless, and was
constantly fed by the sight of the blue mountains,
that served as a link to bind her heart to her child-
hood's home. To her only living child—a girl of
some ten or eleven years—she often spoke of Cefn-
Lee, nestled in the shadow of those great mountains, and screened from the wild west wind that
swept in from the sea, until to the child's vivid
imagination Cefn-Lee seemed a veritable garden

of Eden, where blight and winter and cold could never come.

She laid her work in her lap at length, and called, gently, " Cricket, darling."

"Yes, mother," the girl answered, coming at the same moment to the open door.

" Come an' look at the mountains, honey," and without a word the child came and stood by her mother's side, and turned her face to the glorious west. The sun had disappeared by this, but the sky shone up behind the hills like a sheet of burnished gold, and against this glorious background the long mountain range stood out in clear relief, tipped with a purple line, as though a rainbow had fallen and bent itself to the irregularities of the mountain peaks.

For a while neither Cricket nor her mother spoke ; both were entranced with the beauty of the scene. Cricket was the first to break the silence. " I should like to see Cefn-Lee," she said. " It must be all light and gold on the other side of the mountains."

" That iss becauss the sky looks close to the mount'ins," the mother answered, who never was able to get out of her Welsh accent. "But if you wass there, Cricket, the sky would be just as far away as it iss here."

"I don't see how that could be," Cricket answered, somewhat puzzled.

"Ah well, honey, you shall go there some day," the mother answered, with a little sigh.

"Shall I, mother?" the child replied, with a smile; "you have said that often an' often."

"But I mean it all the same; an' it's not been my fault, darlin', that we have not gone."

"Will it cost much to go?" Cricket asked after a little pause.

"Yes, honey; several shillin's. And your father thinks we can't afford it, and I don't like to say anything to him, for he begins to complain about hiss wages, and wants to go to Liverpool, where he says he could get heaps more."

"And wouldn't you like to go to Liverpool, mother?" Cricket asked.

"No, darlin'; it iss a wicked place, with drink shops at nearly every corner, so I've heard, an' bad people all about. Oh no, Cricket, I should dread goin' to Liverpool, for your father's sake."

"But if he would be able to get lots of money," Cricket answered, "wouldn't that be jolly!"

"Money isn't everything, honey," the mother answered with a sigh; "lots of things iss better than money, an' we haf enough to keep us from want."

"But if we had lots more," Cricket replied, "we should be able to go to Cefn-Lee."

"If we had lots more *here*, Cricket; but lots more in Liverpool iss very different. We should haf rent to pay there, and haf no gardin', nor green fields, and never a sight of the mount'ins; and your father would be surrounded by public-houses and bad people. Oh no, Cricket! I'd rather live here, though we hadn't haff the money."

Cricket did not reply. She stood watching the fading light over the mountain tops. She did not share her mother's feelings with respect to Liverpool. On the contrary, she thought it would be "just splendid" to live where she would be able to see great ships, and splendid buildings, and streets crowded with well-dressed people, and all the other wonders of city life.

Every now and then, stories reached their quiet

country home of the wonders to be seen in the great city that stood on the farther bank of the Mersey. And Cricket's eyes would grow wide with interest while she listened, and her little heart would flutter with excitement.

Richard Chase—Cricket's father—would listen with stolid indifference, unless some one should happen to speak of the wages that might be earned at the docks, then his heavy stolid face would light up in a moment, and clenching his huge fist, he would grumble out something about " not standing it much longer."

He was in the main a sullen, discontented man, with a fondness for his pipe and mug. If he once got inside the door of an ale-house, he would rarely leave it till all his money was done, and it was the knowledge of this fact that led his wife to turn a deaf ear to all the stories about the splendid wages to be earned at the Liverpool docks, and to steadily oppose his leaving his situation at Scar End Farm.

She knew very well that more money with him would mean more drink, and consequently more trouble for her.

Fortunately for him at present, there was no public-house within two miles of his home, and when his day's work was done he was often too tired to tramp so far. Moreover, his master generally managed somehow to hand over his wages to his (Chase's) wife. Perhaps it was his knowledge of Richard Chase's propensity that led him to do this. The less hard cash he fingered the better it was for him.

It was late on the evening in question when he returned from his work, for the hay-harvest was in full swing, and every hand on the farm was busy till dark. Cricket and her mother had remained under the hawthorn tree till the glow had faded out of the western sky and the far-off mountains had vanished in the gathering gloom. Then they retired into the house, and sat facing each other in the deepening twilight, talking in low earnest tones.

Cricket was her mother's confidant, as well as her mother's joy. All her other children had died in infancy save little Bob, who had reached the age of three ere the angels carried him away to the better home. Martha Chase had never been

quite the same since he died—not that she moped,
or obtruded her grief on either husband or child—
but there was a pathetic look in her eyes that
nothing could chase away, and a sad undertone in
her voice that was always there.

Cricket often caught her with her hands lying
listlessly in her lap, and her eyes fixed on the far-
off hills, and wondered if it were Cefn-Lee of
which her mother was thinking, or of that happier
country still, where little Bob had gone.

In truth, in these days, she oftener thought of
the heavenly country than of Cefn-Lee. A great
piece of her heart was there with her angel boy.
Besides which, her health was very feeble, and
sometimes she felt so weary that she almost longed
for rest.

Cricket never vexed her mother at such times
with idle questions. She loved to see the earnest,
peaceful look that would settle upon her face,
and rightly guessed, that for the time she was
living beyond the care and worry of her daily
life.

But it was not of little Bob or heaven they
talked to-night, but of Cricket's father, of his dis·

c

content with his present lot, and of his growing determination to seek his fortune in the huge wicked city, the smoke of which they could sometimes see darkening the northern sky.

" I think I would rather die than go," she said to Cricket, " for I am sure I should die if I wass to go. I could not lif in the noiss and smoke."

" But you'd soon get used to it," Cricket suggested.

" Oh no, I never should," she answered with a sigh. " I've lif'd all my life among green fields or among the mount'ins, and sometimes now I can hardly get my breath, an' if I wass to go into that smoky city I should choke."

To this Cricket made no answer, and after a while her mother went on again.

" I love the mount'ins, Cricket; they make me think of my father and mother, and home. I don't seem far away when only the beautiful mount'ins stand between, and from their tops it don't seem far to heaven."

A little sigh followed this, and then silence fell between them. They could not see each other's faces now, for all the daylight had faded out of the sky, and the little room was wrapped in complete darkness.

After a while Cricket rose from her chair, and glided up to her mother's side and kissed her. " I think I'll light the lamp now and get father's supper ready," she said, " for he'll soon be home."

" You're a good girl, Cricket," her mother answered. " I'm sorry you haf so much to do. I hope I will be stronger after a while, and then you shall haf easier times."

" I like to be doing," Cricket answered, cheerfully, as she placed the lighted lamp on the table, and then proceeded to make ready for the evening meal.

CHAPTER II.

"'TAINT HOME NO MORE LIKE IT USED TO BE."

" Thou art gone home !   Oh ! early crowned and blest ;
  Where could the love of that deep heart find rest
          With aught below ?
  Thou must have seen rich dream by dream decay—
  All the bright rose-leaves drop from life away—
          Thrice blest to go !"

HEMANS.

CARCELY had Cricket got the supper ready when Richard Chase returned from his work, hungry, cross, and tired. The sight and smell of the ham rasher and fried potato, however, that Cricket had cooked to a nicety, mollified him a little, and with the exception of kicking the cat to the other end of the room, he gave no further evidence of his ill-humour until the meal was ended.   As soon as that was over, however, he turned sullenly, almost savagely, towards his wife, and said—

"Look you here, missus, I ain't agoin' to stand this no longer."

"Stand what, Richard?" she asked, meekly enough, though she was almost certain what was coming.

"You know weal eno'," he answered with a snarl, "an' if it hadn't been for you I shouldn't have stood it so long as I've done."

"What I've done, Richard, I've done for the best," she replied, "and I haf nothing to blame myself with in that matter."

"It's a pity everybody ain't as good an opinion of yer as ye have of yourself," was his reply. "Any road, it's my opinion that for years ye've just stood right in the way of our gettin' on."

"I'm sorry you think so, Richard," was her only answer.

"Well, I do think so," he answered with a scowl, "and what's more I can prove it."

"In which way?" she asked.

"In this way," he answered. "Only this very afternoon, Ned Tipple came into the hay-field in which we was workin' in the blazin' sun and feeling as dry as a lime-burner's shoe, for Greg has cut down the beer to a gallon a day each, this year, as if we were childern instead of full-grown men. A purty pass the world is a comin' to; next thing we'll be put on cold water or ginger pop."

Here followed an awkward pause of several seconds, during which Chase stared stupidly, first at his wife, and then at Cricket. It was very evident, in spite of his complaint, that he had taken during the day quite as much beer as was good for him, and a little more.

"Blame me," he said at length, with a loud hiccough, "if I ain't clean forgot what I was a goin' to say."

"Oh well, never mind, Richard," said his wife, "you can tell us to-morrow."

"Can I?" he said with a leer. "But s'pose I don't choose to. You think you're a goin' to get my secrets out of me, do yer? Let me tell yer Dick Chase is none so green."

At this he smiled complacently, evidently being of the opinion that he had scored a point, and getting up from his chair he proceeded to light his pipe at the grate. This done, he returned to his seat and for a while smoked in silence.

Cricket busied herself in clearing the supper table, while her mother went on with her sewing, but every now and then casting anxious glances at her husband, who smoked defiantly in the corner.

"You should ha' seen Ned Tipple this afternoon," he burst out at length; "he looked quite the swell an' no mistake: a perfect gent."

"Indeed," said his wife.

"Ay! He had a green-an'-yellow waistcoat; an' four rows o' white buttons on it, a blue hankicher round 'is neck wi' red spots on it, a brown velvet jacket an' a real seal-skin cap. I tell you he was got up 'quite regardless,' as he said his-sel, an' no flummery."

"What is he doing to dress so fine?" Cricket asked, after a short pause.

"That is what I'm a comin' to," was the reply. "He's workin' in Liverpool at the Docks, an' arnin' six and seven bob a day reg'lar, an' he says, I'm a fool to slave on a farm for fourteen bob a week as I'm a doin'."

"But you forget that we've no rent to pay," said his wife, "an' that we haf a large gardin where we can grow all our potatoes, an' that we are able to feed our own pig, and lots of other privileges."

"Ay, the pri'lege o' livin' in a thatch'd hut," he grumbled, "that farmer Greg 'ud be 'shamed to house his cows in."

"But its warm, an' comfortable an' clean, for all that," replied his wife, "an' we have sweet air, and pure water, an' cool shade when it's hot, an' the far-off mount'ins to feast our eyes on all the while."

"Hang the mountains !" he sneered ; "yer talk as if the mountains were o' use to us. They gives us neither vittels or clothes, so what's the use ? "

She made no reply to this. She felt that no good could come of arguing with him in his present mood. Nevertheless, she resolved not to yield until she was compelled. She did not try to hide from herself the fact that her husband's work was almost slavery : that the days were long and the pay small, while there was not the slightest prospect of his bettering his position, however long he might remain. Yet in the past they had not been on the whole unhappy. Though sorely pinched sometimes for money, they had never known the meaning of actual want. If meat was scarce—as it sometimes happened to be—there were always plenty of potatoes and bread to which they could turn, while fuel could be had for the gathering.

But more than all this, to her, was the fact that here her husband was subjected to few temptations. No flaring drink-shops stood by the roadside as he returned from his labour. No idle and dissolute companions were here to tempt him into evil paths. He spent his days in the quiet fields, where nearly every influence that touched him was sweet and pure. His ears, instead of being polluted by ribald songs, were charmed by the singing of happy birds. His eyes, instead of gazing on wretchedness and vice, saw only Nature's unstained beauty: the quiet fields and shining meadow pools, the yellow hillsides where the billowy corn-fields glinted golden in the sunshine, the wooded uplands where the summer winds made dreamy music among the trees, and the far-off mountains rearing their soft crests to heaven.

True, her husband professed to despise all these things, yet for all that, she could not but believe that they did him good in spite of himself, elevated his thought and feeling in a way he did not know, and saved him from utter debasement of spirit.

She knew his weaknesses better than he knew them himself, for he was not a man given to reflection or introspection. He never thought of danger or temptation; in his desire to remove to Liverpool, never thought of his child or of the influence such a change might have upon her life. All he thought of was the wages : thirty-five or forty shillings a week seemed positive riches. He would be able to dress on Sundays equal to Ned Tipple, and have a jollification every Saturday night.

Hence nothing that his wife might say could shake him in his resolution. He knew that she would hold out as long as she could, but when she saw how determined he was, he had no doubt she would yield sooner or later. He did not want to go against her will if that could be avoided, but if it couldn't be avoided it would have to be endured, for go he would, and she would have to see who was master.

Very little more was said that evening. Richard Chase having "had his say," smoked his pipe in silence, and then, without a word or a good-night kiss, retired to rest. Cricket and her mother soon followed his example ; and in a very few minutes silence and darkness had possession of the little cot.

Richard Chase had his way, and sooner than he expected, and when the time of his departure was fixed no word of opposition or remonstrance was raised. By the middle of October he was settled in Liverpool, in a narrow dingy street known as Cooper's Row, and had found pretty regular work at the Docks.

It was a bright though chilly morning when the little family left their quiet Cheshire home, for the great noisy city that poor Martha Chase had always cherished such a horror of. Perhaps it was well she was not there to see the break-up of the little home that she loved so much, and that she had striven so hard to keep bright and clean. Two months before, and just three days after little Jack was born, she quietly passed away into the silent land.

Her death was as unexpected as it was sudden.

Old Mary Pugh, who was both doctor and nurse, had declared not two hours previously that she was "doing splendidly." Martha Chase herself seemed to have had no suspicion that her end was so near ; while Cricket had found a new joy in her little baby-brother, and in her heart there was no thought of trouble.

So without warning the angel of death came into that lowly home, and touched the mother's heart, and it grew gently still. There was no struggle ; no spasm of pain swept across her face. For an hour she had lain with eyes closed as if asleep. The old nurse, with noiseless hand, had drawn the curtains around the bed, and then had opened the window to air the room. The afternoon was warm and sultry, with scarcely a sound to break the stillness. Outside, the stream rippled along with gentlest murmur, and now and then voices and sounds from the distant corn-fields floated softly on the air, but these alone disturbed the quiet of the afternoon. Cricket was seated under the hawthorn tree with a story-book in her lap, but with her eyes fixed on the far-off mountains. She was too happy to read. Her heart was so full of peace

that it was a perfect joy to sit still, in the shadow
of the tree, and feel upon her brow the warm soft
breath of heaven, and watch the billowy corn-fields
rolling away in the level distance, and see rising up
beyond the plain the glorious mountains clothed in
a thin raiment of purple haze.

Suddenly she was startled by the nurse's voice,
calling from the open window—

" Cricket, child, run an' fetch yer father, quick ;
yer mother's taken worse sudden."

" Taken worse ? " cried Cricket, with alarm,
scarcely realising what the nurse's words implied.

" Ay, child, quick, an' ask yer father to send
somebody for the doctor."

Without another word Cricket leaped the brook
that separated the garden from the field, and went
bounding on like a startled hare.   She knew where
her father was working, and so made straight for
the corn-field, climbing the hedges without a
thought of the thorns, and clearing the ditches
with a bound that was a surprise to herself.

What a change a few moments had wrought !
Five minutes ago she was sitting under the tree
without a thought of trouble, now her heart was

almost bursting with pain and anxiety. It seemed a strange Providence that could dash the child's joy so suddenly and completely.

In the journey home she could not keep pace with her father, for she had run herself completely out of breath. At the door the nurse met her and told her all, and Cricket knew that she and her little baby-brother were motherless.

"You mustn't fret any more'n you can 'elp," said Nurse Pugh. "An' yer must keep up as well as yer can for the baby's sake."

Cricket broke down completely at this, and began to sob outright.

"It's very 'ard, I know," said the nurse, kindly. "But you must think how she's better off."

"Oh yes, I know she's better off," said Cricket, brokenly, "but somehow that don't make it any easier to bear."

"She'd 'a had to go sooner or later," was the reply; "and she went without no pain. It weren't 'ard dyin' for her at all."

"Oh, I'm glad she didn't suffer!" said Cricket.

"She just opened her eyes an' looked up as though she were a lookin' through the roof," was the reply. " An' then she smiled ever so sweetly, and whispered, 'Bob, darlin', I'm comin''; and with a little sigh she were gone. I knowed it were all over when I called yer to fetch yer father, but I didn't want to frighten yer too much."

In the days that followed the care of the baby proved a great blessing to Cricket. For his sake she was compelled to rouse herself, and yet when she looked into his round blue eyes, and thought how he would never know a mother's love or care, it nearly broke her heart.

Richard Chase seemed like a man stunned for two or three days, and scarcely spoke a word to any one. He took no notice of the baby at all, and very little of Cricket. Whether his grief was very acute or not, it was impossible to say.

After the funeral, however, he recovered himself rapidly, and soon began to talk again about going to Liverpool. Indeed, he seemed to think that he had a double reason now for taking this step.

" 'Taint home no more like it used to be," he said to Cricket, after his wife had been dead a month and the nurse had left. " An' 'taint a place noather for you to be all alone day after day an' not a na'bor near an' comin' on winter too, with long, dark evenin's. Now, in Liverpool 'twill be very differn't : there you'll 'ave na'bors all round, front an' behind an' both sides at once. It'll be a mighty sight better nor living 'ere."

To this Cricket raised no objection. Indeed, she had none to raise. She felt the truth of what her father had said : that the place was home no more like it used to be. She missed her mother everywhere. It seemed to her as if all the music and sunshine had gone out of the place, and there were times when she felt that it would be a relief to get away to new scenes, and to a different kind of life.

So it came about that on the following month the little home was broken up, and the furniture carefully packed was sent off to Liverpool, No. 13, Cooper's Row. Ned Tipple—who had married a first cousin of Richard Chase—took the house for them next door to his own.

Cricket had no regrets until she saw the cottage dismantled ; then all her old love for the place came back again, and she sat down on a box with little Jack in her arms, and burst into tears. She

felt almost thankful now that her mother was dead,
the sight of the old home all bare and desolate
would have broken her heart.

Cricket never forgot that chilly October morning, when she walked down the garden path for
the last time. In this little cottage she had been
born, and here she had lived all her life. Every
bush and bank and tree was as familiar to her as
her father's face. Would she ever like another
place so well, she wondered, or would any other
place ever seem to her like home ?

" I wish now," she said to her father in low tones,
" that we wer'n't going away."

But he did not hear, or if he heard he vouchsafed
no reply.

At the garden gate she paused a few moments
for a last look. The sun was shining brightly.
But the chill of coming winter was on all the scene.
Even while she looked, the wind shook the syca·
more at the end of the house, and the broad
brown leaves fluttered silently to the earth. The
brook—swollen with recent rains—seemed to murmur with sadder tones, while the October wind had
a mournful tone in it that smote her to the heart.

D

Suddenly she could not see any more for the tears, and choking back the sobs she turned away her head, and followed after her father with swift and resolute steps.

Billy knocking at the door.—p. 42

CHAPTER III.

"LET US GO BACK AGAIN."

> " Oh, pardon, that in crowds a while
>   I waste one thought I owe to thee,
> And, self-condemned, appear to smile,
>   Unfaithful to thy memory."
>
> BYRON.

T sight of Cooper's Row, Cricket's heart sank within her.

"Oh, father," she said, "there must be some mistake."

"Mistake about what?" he grumbled.

"About the place," she answered. "This cannot be Cooper's Row, the place we are going to live. Oh, father, we can never stay in a horrible dirty place like this."

"Don't begin to grumble fust thing," he snarled; "t' place is right eno'. Did yer expect a thatched cottage and fields all round it?"

"Oh no, I did not expect that," she answered, with tears in her eyes; "but I didn't expect this. Look at the windows, and the doorsteps, and the children, and everything. Oh, father, let us go back again."

"Don't be a fool?" he snapped. "Ye'll soon get used to it, and when yer gets to know the people ye'll be 'appy as a queen."

Cricket made no further reply. She knew it was of no use, but her heart was aching fit to break, and her eyes so full of tears that she could scarce see anything.

During all the journey hither she had been full of excitement, not unmixed with pleasure. To travel by train was a new experience in her life, and as the trees and cottages and fields went scudding by on either side her spirits rose perceptibly.

"Oh, this is just splendid!" she said to herself, giving baby Jack an extra kiss by way of giving vent to her excitement.

And when at length they reached Birkenhead, and embarked on one of the huge ferry-boats that ply on the river, her excitement knew no bounds.

To sit still was an utter impossibility; up and

down the long stretch of deck she paced with the baby in her arms, her eyes wide open with wonder, her lips apart, her face aglow with pleasure.

The passengers that crowded on the deck to enjoy the bright sunshine and the keen fresh breeze that swept down the river, could scarcely repress a smile as they watched her pacing up and down the deck. They saw by her simple and homely attire, and her sunburnt cheeks, that she was fresh from the country. A group of empty-headed dandies tried to make fun at her expense, but she did not heed them, and their efforts miserably failed. She had no eyes for anything on board, no ears for the voices around her. All her attention was fixed on the great shining river, crowded with the ships of all nations.

She had often heard of the River Mersey, and of the great vessels that ploughed its waters; but her most vivid dreams had never pictured a scene like this. She wondered how her father could sit down there on the lower deck quietly smoking his pipe, and taking no notice of what was passing around him, while she was thrilling to the finger-tips with pleasure and excitement.

Oh, how the waters sparkled and shone in the sunshine, and stretched away right and left as far as eye could reach! How nobly the vessel breasted the waves—and big ones they seemed to her—rolling in from the sea, and tossed them right and left in its conscious strength, while the paddle-wheels caught them up again and churned them into foam!

Never in all her life had she known an experience so exhilarating as this; even the vessel, it seemed to her, caught her enthusiasm, and panted and throbbed beneath her feet like a thing of life.

Brook Cottage was forgotten now, and all the regrets of the morning were over and past. If this was coming to Liverpool, it exceeded her brightest dreams. Alas! poor child, how little she knew of what was in store for her!

The short voyage across the river came to an end all too soon, and then, and then—

But what need is there that we should describe the events of that day in greater detail? That Cricket's heart should sink at sight of Cooper's Row none can wonder. After the shining river and the sweet breath of the sea, the squalor and dirt and smoke of the gloomy court were positively sickening. But Cricket choked back her sobs as best she could, and resolved, for her father's sake, and for the sake of little Jack, she would make the best of it, and try to be cheerful and content.

Some fresh paper had been put on the walls, and when the furniture had been properly arranged, the place began to look a little more like home; and Cricket began to hope that life in Liverpool might not be so bad as she at first feared it would be.

Mrs. Tipple, her father's cousin and next-door neighbour, seemed quite disposed to be friendly, and told Cricket that if she wanted help at any time, she would be only too glad to help her. Indeed, Cricket could not see how she would be able to get along at all without help of some kind; for though she was a strong, healthy girl, and would have passed anywhere for being fourteen years of age, yet to keep a house clean, to do all the cooking, and look after a baby at the same time, involved an amount of labour that she felt certain she could not accomplish.

Hence Mrs. Tipple quite won Cricket's heart by her offer of help, and Cricket told her, with tears in her eyes, that she could never be thankful enough as long as she lived.

Richard Chase had no difficulty in getting work, for trade was brisk at the time, and labourers in great demand. He found the work very trying for the first few weeks, and when he returned in the evenings he complained once or twice of being so stiff and sore that he could hardly move. But the large wages he received each Saturday seemed to atone for any discomfort he might have suffered during the week, and he jingled the money in his pocket with a sense of great satisfaction.

So the weeks passed away, and winter came on apace. Baby Jack lived and throve in spite of fog and skimmed milk, and Cricket was getting accustomed to the surrounding squalor and dirt, and to the sight of children in rags and tatters, with bare feet and hungry, wolfish faces.

Her fears respecting her father, with which her mother had inspired her, did not seem at all likely to be realised. Only once had he been the worse for drink since they came to Cooper's Row, and that was through following the advice of Ned Tipple, which he declared he would not do again.

Cricket found, as the weeks slipped away, that she had no cause of complaint at all. He was more than usually kind to her and little Jack, and allowed her, without any grumbling, all the money she required for household purposes.

That he should spend his Saturday evening at some public-house with his mates, was a matter that occasioned her no surprise, and little regret, so long as he came home sober. Hence, on the whole, she was fairly content. Now and then during the dark foggy days of November, when the court was wrapped in darkness, denser than she had ever known in the country at midnight— she longed for the sweet breath of the fields and hills, and for the quiet and peace of her early home. But she crushed back the longing as best she could, and allowed no word of complaint to escape her lips.

With the advent of December people began to talk freely about the coming Christmas, and " goose clubs " were being arranged for at nearly all the public-houses in the neighbourhood.

" We have rare times o' it at Christmas," said Ned Tipple to Richard Chase one evening in the early part of December, as they sat together over the fire at No. 13, Cooper's Row.

" Indeed ! " grunted Chase.

" Ay, an' we keep the thing up too," was the answer. " We take the round of the na'bors, an' keep goin' to the small."

At this speech Chase took the pipe out of his mouth and blinked stupidly.

"Well, hang me," he said at length, " if I can see what business it is o' yourn, whether yer na'bors are round or square, small or big."

Tipple laughed immoderately at this, much to Chase's annoyance.

" Well," he said, looking fiercely at his neighbour, " an' what is there to laugh at ? "

" Excuse me, Chase," said Tipple, good-humouredly, "but you're so awfully downy an' tender, that I were taken off the hooks for a moment. But I was goin' to tell you 'bout our Christmas do's."

" Well, plough ahead then," said Chase, " an' don't go scudderin' all round the field."

" That's good for you, anyhow," said Tipple. " But look 'ere, Chase, you'll 'ave to be like the other chaps, an' join the clubs, and pay yer mite to the sinkin' fund."

"I wish ye'd talk plain English, any road," answered Chase. "A man o' your eddication oughter be able to speak correck."

"Well, yer see," answered Tipple, "goose clubs is all the order at Christmas time. You'll not object to a goose for your Christmas dinner, I guess."

"I reckon not," was the reply.

"Very good," said Tipple; "but wot's vittels worth without summat to wash it down?"

"True for you," said Chase.

"Very good! We forms a sinkin' fund; ten or a dozen o' us drops in so much every week. By Christmas we gits a gallon o' real Scotch; do yer take?"

"Ay."

"Very good again! Wot's the use o' vittels and drink without a place to take 'em in comfort?"

"True once more," said Chase.

"Very good for the fourth time," answered Tipple. "The pubs close at 'leven; consekently we arrange to meet at each other's houses. Laws nor peelers can't touch us there. We do the thing neat, an' break up early."

" Early ? " said Chase. " How so ? "

" Early in the morning, to be sure. Now you take. Are you game, like the rest ? "

" I'll think 'bout it," said Chase. " There ain't no hurry, I s'pose ? "

" That's just what there is," was the reply. " In most places the game's in full swing already. But I'm not agoin' to press it on yer. It's no gain to me. We keeps the thing select as far as the sinkin' fund goes. You've the chance of joinin' 'cause as 'ow yer a friend o' mine. There's plenty I can tell yer who'd jump at the honour."

" In that case yer can book me," said Chase.

" Right you are," was the answer. " I want the other fellows to see ye're not so downy as yer look. Lots of 'em are getting to think yer no game."

" Is that so ? " said Chase, clenching his fists savagely.

" Ay, it's so, but then who can wonder ? You've kept yerself so much to yerself that they've scarce had a chance of knowin' yer."

To this Chase made no reply, and soon after the two men went out together.

" Ye'd better enter yer name at once," Tipple had suggested, and to this Richard Chase raised no objection.

Cricket, who had been busy in trying to get little Jack to sleep, had only heard parts of the conversation, but what she had heard occasioned her no anxiety whatever.

As the evening wore away, however, her feelings underwent a very decided change. Hour after hour passed away till the clock was close on the stroke of midnight, and still her father had not come. By the smouldering embers she had sat in the dim light of a solitary candle, waiting and listening, and now a great fear had crept into her heart, that her father had come to grief. For once Cooper's Row was quiet, no single voice, nor solitary footstep broke the silence ; under its coverlet of fog and smoke the dingy court was asleep.

At length from a neighbouring church tower the huge bell clanged out the hour of midnight ; a few minutes later, heavy and unsteady steps were heard in the court outside. Cricket sprang to her feet in a moment, but before she could reach the door it was thrust wide open, and her father staggered helplessly into the room.

In his drunken bewilderment he had lost himself in the network of streets and courts, and had been wandering aimlessly about for the best part of an hour. As a consequence he was in a worse temper than Cricket had ever known him. Several times he tried to strike her, and would have done so had he been able to aim straight.

About one o'clock, however, he fell asleep on the floor, and Cricket, covering him with an old rug and placing a pillow under his head, crept sadly and silently upstairs and nestled down by the side of little Jack. It was a long time, however, before she fell asleep. Her thoughts troubled her in a way she could hardly understand. It was not the first by many times that she had seen her father the worse for drink, and she had never troubled very much about it before.

"It's being skear'd at his being out so late that's fidgeted me, I expect," she said to herself at length; "an' so I'll try to forget it."

In this she succeeded after a while, though her

sleep was anything but sound, and troubled dreams haunted her all the night.

Richard Chase seemed little the worse next morning, and in the evening he was quite ready to respond to the invitation of Ned Tipple and pay another visit to the "Royal George." Indeed, the goose club and the sinking fund made constant demand upon his time, so much so, that he scarcely ever had an evening at home now with his children.

As the days passed on, Cricket got to almost hate the sight of Ned Tipple. His knock at the door just after supper meant to her another lonely and anxious evening. For Ned Tipple's wife went "spreeing on her own account," as she termed it, so that Cricket could never count upon her company.

As Christmas drew nearer Cricket's heart sank more and more. She could no longer hide from herself the fact that her father was getting into bad ways. All her old fears—born of talk with her mother—came back to her again with tenfold force. For five or six weeks after coming to Liverpool he had been all that she could desire. But since that night when he had joined the goose club and the

sinking fund, all had been changed. He scarcely
seemed like the same man.

It is true he was rarely out after eleven o'clock,
and rarely so much under the influence of drink
but that he knew quite well what he was about.
But what pained Cricket most was, that he was
never at his ease when at home, while the excite-
ments of the " Royal George," whatever they might
be, seemed to get a greater hold upon him day by
day.

Time after time she heard vague hints about
having " won " so much, and at other times about
" losing heavily," until the conviction was forced
upon her that the goose club and the drink were
not the only attractions at the " Royal George."

Christmas Eve came at length. Richard Chase
was early attired in his Sunday best, for the
drawing was to take place that evening.

At Cricket's request he promised to bring home
the goose early, for she wanted to get it properly
dressed and ready for cooking, so that there might
be no delay on the morrow.

He was in great good-humour, and even chucked
Cricket playfully under the chin before he went

out. "We'll 'ave a rare feast together, to-morrow, my gal," he said, "so 'ave everything in readiness."

Alas for Cricket! Alas for him! Hour after hour she waited, racked with alternate hopes and fears. Many footsteps echoed in the court outside, but his was not amongst them. She watched the hands of the clock creep slowly round and round the dial, until her very brain seemed to be on fire. And so the evening passed and midnight came, and the night passed and the morning dawned, and still he had not come.

CHAPTER IV.

"I DON'T KNOW WHO YOU ARE."

> " Freeze, freeze, thou bitter sky,
>   That dost not bite so nigh
>   As benefits forgot :
>   Though thou the waters warp,
>   Thy sting is not so sharp
>   As friend remembered not."
>
> SHAKESPEARE.

HE church clock had some time ago clanged forth the hour of midnight. The hum of voices and the echo of footsteps had gradually grown less and less, till now, not only Cooper's Row, but the busier Bunter Street, out of which it opened, had grown perfectly still. Farther away, along the great thoroughfare of Scotland Road, the rattle of a cab might be heard at intervals, with now and then the laugh or shout of some belated toper reeling homewards through the deserted streets, but, with these exceptions, the night was not only cold and dark, but still.

Sitting by the merest ghost of a fire, with her hands clasped, her face white and haggard, and her great, round eyes full of terror, was Cricket, anxiously waiting the unsteady step of her father. He had forgotten his promise again, as he had more than once done of late, and she knew now that when he did return, he would not only be helpless, but angry. He had never been one of the sweetest-tempered men, but of late, when in drink, he had become positively unkind ; so much so, that while she longed for, she almost dreaded, his return.

At length a quick, soft patter of feet in the court outside startled her, and the next moment there came a faint rat-tat on the door. Instantly Cricket rushed to the door, and opened it. On the threshold stood a ragged, barefoot, and hungry-looking lad of about her own age, with a large brown paper parcel under his arm.

" Please, marm," he stammered, " be you ex-pectin' a bird at this 'ere 'ouse ? "

" I hardly know what you mean," said Cricket, somewhat taken aback

"This are number thirteen, aint it?" the lad asked.

"Yes, this is number thirteen," Cricket answered, in some confusion; "but I don't know who you are."

"No, most likely yer don't," he answered, with a grin. "It 'ud be mighty queer if yer did, though I'm know'd about 'ere pretty middlin', 'specially by the peelers—begs parding, marm, the pleece I means."

During this speech Cricket had time to recover herself a little, and to take stock of her midnight visitor.

He was by no means ill-looking; his face, though thin and hunger-lined, was frank and open; his eyes were large and bright, with a constantly changing expression, now of suspicion, now of cunning, and now brimming over with mirth. His hair was brown, and thickly curling all over his head. He wore no cap nor shoes, while his clothes were ragged beyond description.

On the whole, however, Cricket was pleased with his appearance, and, without any further hesitancy, asked him if he would come in for a minute out of the cold. She felt certain that her father would not remain away much longer, and anything that would help to pass away the time would be welcome.

"Yer very kind, marm," the lad replied. "An if ye'll give me a crust or a copper, for bringin' yer the bird, I'd be mighty thankful."

"Are you very hungry?" Cricket asked, eyeing him closely.

"Well, rather, marm," he replied, with a grin that brightened all his face. "Folks ha' been so full o' their own Christmas, that they've forgot 'ow I were as empty as a drum."

"Then you'd better sit in this chair till my father comes," Cricket answered. "I'm expecting him every minute, and you can be eatin' this while you wait," and Cricket placed before him a large piece of bread and cheese.

For two or three minutes the lad ate ravenously and in silence, then, turning his bright eyes full on Cricket, he said,—

"I guess your father'll never come 'ome to-night."

"Not come home to-night!" said Cricket, while a startled look swept over her face.

"Well, I'm thinkin' not," the lad answered, in tones that had a touch of pity in them.

"Do you know my father, then?" Cricket asked; "or what is it that you do know?"

"Well, I don't know yer father, to begin wi'," was the answer, "an' what I do know aint much; but I'll tell yer the top an' bottom on it, an' then perhaps yer can make summat out o' it for yerself."

"Be quick about it then, please," said Cricket.

"Well, the truth is," the boy answered, "I were dead-beat and ready to drop. So I just creeps up a hentry off Scotlan' Road, and gets into a hempty barrel, anywheres, yer see, to be hout o' the wind and cold. Well, marm, I 'adn't a been there many minutes when I 'ears a great row just at th mouth o' the hentry. Somebody said as 'ow somebody else 'ad got his goose, an' then they begins a fightin'. I could 'ear that plain enough. Well, that went on for some time, and then the bobbies drops on 'em sudden, an' there was just a scrabble an' no mistake. Whistles were a blowin' and blows a knockin' round pretty general, and durin' this scrabble somethin' were throw'd by somebody, an'

drops right on to the barrel I were in. Well, the
bobbies, as far as I could make out, marched off
one or two o' the men to the pleece-station. After
that it were a bit quiet, an' I 'ears one o' the men
as were left axin what 'ad become o' Dick's bird,
but nobody seemed to know; but as they were a
clearin' off, I 'ears one on 'em say he guessed there'd
be no goose for dinner at 13 Cooper's Row this
Christmas. Well, I lies luff for a long time, till all
were quiet, then I steals out o' the barrel, picks up
this 'ere goose, finds as 'ow it were nothin' as I
could eat, an' so makes up my mind to bring it
'ere, thinkin' that likely I'd get a copper for my
trubble or a snack to eat."

During the delivery of this long speech Cricket's
anxiety steadily increased.

"Do you really think," she asked, at length,
"that my father's been taken to prison?"

"Oh no, not to prison, marm, on'y to the pleece-
station."

"But perhaps you're mistaken," Cricket answered, with tears in her eyes. "Oh, I hope you
are, perhaps 'twern't father after all."

"Well, marm, I don't know nothin' more'n I've

told yer, an' I'm werry sorry to bring bad news, but I put it together this way, that one o' the men as were walked off were called Dick, and that he lived at 13 Cooper's Row, an' that finding he were nabbed, he just flings away his goose so that the pleece shouldn't get it, nor nobody else."

"Well, it was very kind of you to bring the goose here," said Cricket, huskily, after a pause.

"Well, marm, yer see, I couldn't eat it, that were the reason, an' I thought, pr'aps, I'd get somethin' for doin' it, an', yer see, I were right."

"And if the parcel had been something else— something you could eat—you'd not have brought it ?" said Cricket, feeling considerably shocked at the lad's candid admission of his motives.

"Well, I rather think I shouldn't," was the ready and good-humoured answer. "Yer wouldn't take me to be so jolly green as that, would yer ?"

"But if you knew who the parcel belonged to, and kept it yourself, that would be very wicked," said Cricket.

He laughed at that, with a curious twinkle in his eye. "I don't know what 'wicked' are," he said, "but I knows what it are to be 'ungry."

"But to keep what you know belongs to some-body else is as bad as stealin'," said Cricket.

"But what is little chaps to do as aint got *nothin'* o' their own?" he asked.

This seemed to puzzle Cricket for a moment. Then she answered, "You've done the right thing to-night, an' when you take people what belongs to 'em, they will give you something for it."

"Sometimes they will," he answered dubiously "'an sometimes they won't. In any case it's risky, an' the best way is, if yer gets hold o' anything as is good, to eat it an' so make sure of it."

"Oh no," said Cricket, "that aint right at all. Folks should be honest if they starve."

"Neither on 'em are werry easy," was the answer. "I've tried 'em both."

"Have you tried to starve?" said Cricket, in tones of surprise.

"Ay, lots o' times," was the answer. "Yer see there aint no 'elp for it when yer can't get no vittels either by 'ook or by crook."

"But don't your father an' mother give you all you want?" Cricket asked.

"I ain't got no furnitur' o' that sort," was the answer.

"No father nor mother?"

"No, none on 'em," he answered, with a shake of his head.

"Then where do you live?" Cricket asked in surprise.

"Don't live nowhere in pertickler, marm, an' anywheres as 'appens to be a hopenin'."

"An' have you no house of your own, nor bed, nor any home?"

"No, marm, nothin' o' th' sort. I used to 'ave afore mother skeddadled, but that's nigh two years ago now."

"Is your mother dead?" Cricket asked, sadly.

"Dunno, marm; she hooked it one mornin' without sayin' nothin' to nobody, an' she aint turned up since; she may be dead, she may be in gaol, she may ha' got wed again, she may be in the workhus; there's no knowin' nothin' for sartin', marm."

Here was a revelation of Liverpool life that took Cricket completely by surprise. For a while she did not speak again, while the lad began to pick up carefully the crumbs of bread and cheese that remained on the table.

Cricket was getting thoroughly interested too. So much so, that she forgot in some measure her anxiety respecting her father.

At length she asked, "What is your name? you've not told me that yet."

"Lor," he laughed, "that are a caution; wot a 'ole in my manners to be sure. My name's Billy. Wot's your name, if I aint too bold in axin'?"

"My name is Cricket," she answered, colouring a little.

"Treacle," he laughed; "what a name!"

"It aint my real name," she said, in some little confusion; "my real name is Caroline; but I had a little brother once called Bob, and he couldn't say Caroline. He used to call me Crickin at first, and then he got into the way of calling me Cricket. Then father and mother began to call me Cricket also, an' now everybody calls me Cricket, an' it seems as if it was my real name."

"Well, it aint at all bad when yer get a bit used to it," he answered; "but lor, wot's the odds what one's name is."

"No, it don't matter much," said Cricket. "But what are you called besides Billy?"

"Billy Walton," he answered, quickly.

Then there was a long pause, and Cricket heaved a big sigh, for her thoughts had again turned to her father. She would have made inquiries at the Tipples, next door, but they had gone out early in the evening, locking the door after them, and they had evidently not returned yet; at any rate she had heard no sound.

Billy sat as close up to the fire as he could get, but he kept his large brown eyes steadily fixed on Cricket. He thought he had never seen a girl before with so kind and good a face, and he wondered whether she would offer him a corner by the fire for the night, or whether she would send him forth into the street to pass the night in the wind and cold.

Cricket was sorely puzzled also to know what to do. If Billy had not so readily betrayed his moral laxity she would not have hesitated a moment. But here was a lad who didn't know what being wicked was, and who, according to his own confession, had no strict sense of honesty, and of the

rights of other people. If she allowed him to stay
in the house, he might walk off with everything he
could lay hands on before morning, and then how
her father would blame her, and how she would
blame herself. And yet to turn the poor boy into
the wintry street seemed to her to be positively
cruel. Under the circumstances, she was quite at a
loss what to do for the best.

At length she said, abruptly, "Do you ever steal,
Billy?"

"What are steal?" he asked.

"Why, take things that are not yours," she
said.

"In course I does," he said, with a grin; "wot's
I to do? If I takes anythink it must belong to
somebody else, 'cause as 'ow I aint got nothink
o' my own."

"Oh, Billy," she said, and the tears sprang into
her eyes in a moment, "then I can't allow you to
stay here; I'm very sorry, Billy."

"Oh, yer needn't be sorry, marm," he said, a
little bit huskily, "ye've been very good, an' it's
wot I'm used to, everybody sarves me the same,"
and he got up from the chair to go. Outside the

wind wailed dismally up the court, and rattled the window and door as it went sweeping past. Cricket's heart smote her as she listened. But there seemed no help for it. She held out her hand to shake hands with him as he passed, but he did not heed it.

"Good night, Billy," she said.

"Good night, marm," he answered, but he did not lift his eyes to hers. He reached the door and placed his hand upon the latch, then turned to her and said,—

"I 'ope yer father'll come 'ome to yer soon, an' that ye'll 'ave a werry 'appy Chris'mas."

"Thank you, Billy," she answered. "I hope ——" then she stopped suddenly. She felt that it would be mockery to wish this poor homeless, friendless waif a happy Christmas. How could he be happy without a home, or friends, or food, or fire?

"What does yer 'ope, marm?" he asked at length.

"Well," she said in some little confusion, "I wish I could let you stay here all night. But you might——" then she paused again in worse confusion than before.

"Might what?" and he lifted his eyes to hers and looked her straight in the face this time.

"Well, you might steal somethin' before mornin', you know," she answered, bringing out the words slowly.

His eyes dropped suddenly, and for a moment he did not speak. Then raising his eyes again he said,—

"Steal summat from one as has been good to me? No! Billy Walton aint a wiper, nor a snake, nor a cur." And pulling open the door with a jerk he passed quickly out into the wintry street.

Cricket stood stock still for several moments, feeling stunned at the rebuke of Billy's words, then she rushed to the open door and looked eagerly down the court; but he was out of sight.

"Billy," she called, "don't go away, Billy, you shall stay, if you will, an' have some goose for dinner to-morrow."

But there came no response out of the darkness, and after calling again and again and getting no reply, she turned and closed the door behind her and commenced to replenish the fire. That done she rushed up-stairs at a cry from little Jack. He was only hungry, however, and after draining a bottle of milk to the last drop, he fell quietly to sleep again.

Cricket felt that she could not go to bed till her father returned. So she stole quietly down-stairs, and dropped into the rocking-chair in front of the fire. She was feeling very miserable, so miserable indeed that she could keep back the tears no longer, and for a while she sobbed as though her heart would break.

Yet in spite of her trouble, gentle sleep stole over her at length all unconsciously, and when she awoke it was broad day. Outside the air was full of the glad music of Christmas bells, while from the room above little Jack was calling with all his might.

CHAPTER V.

"HE PRIDED HIMSELF ON BEING A 'BROAD' MAN."

> " Words are easy, like the wind,
> Faithful friends are hard to find ;
> Every man will be thy friend,
> Whilst thou hast wherewith to spend ;
> But if store of crowns be scant,
> No man will supply thy want."
>
> SHAKESPEARE.

HEN Billy Walton left the shelter of Cricket's home and plunged into the darkness of the night, he felt, to use his own expression, "Consider'ble snarley." That Cricket should imagine that he would steal anything that belonged to her came as near an insult as anything he had ever experienced. He was not particularly sensitive on a matter of this sort as a general rule ; but Cricket had such a sweet face, and such kind-looking and beautiful eyes, that it was positive pain to him that

F

she should think ill of him. He tried to be angry with her, but could not succeed; her kind eyes seemed to haunt him all the while. Yet, though he heard her call after him, he was too proud to turn back; he only quickened his steps instead, and had soon turned the corner into Bunter Street, and was out of sight and hearing.

Here, however, the wind, that had been gradually rising since midnight, caught him full in the face, and made him look eagerly about for a place of shelter. He had not gone many yards when high above his head the big church-bell struck the hour of two.

For a moment Billy paused and looked up at the tall, tapering spire that shot almost out of sight in the star-lit sky.

Then, with a little sigh, he muttered to himself:

"If I was only a bell, instead o' a little boy, I'd have a 'ouse an' shelter."

Along by the iron railings that fenced the church-yard he moved more slowly till he reached a narrow gate that stood slightly ajar.

"By jabbers, I'll go in 'ere," he said to himself. "Maybe, I may find a snug corner somewheres, for it's bitter cold in this wind."

Directly under the chancel window there was a narrow gap, not much broader than a grave and nearly as deep, leading down to a cellar-room underneath the church, where the heating apparatus was placed, and where also Levi Lobb, the sexton of St. Chad's, kept his brushes, dusters, and gardening tools.

Into this gap Billy had nearly fallen. Luckily, however, he espied his danger in time, and espied also the stone-steps leading down to the cellar-door.

"Glorious!" he ejaculated, as he ran lightly down the stone steps, "I'll be as snug as Moses in there."

Close to the door was a mat, and on this Billy coiled himself up as best he could, tucking his feet underneath him, and wrapping his tattered jacket tightly around his shivering frame.

It was a very poor shelter at best, for though the wind did not touch him here, the night air was piercingly cold. But Billy made the best of it.

"I sha'n't be able to find a better place nor this to-night," he said to himself, "so I'll wait here for the mornin'."

Around the gables of the old church and across the silent graves the wind wailed and moaned, making sad, dreamy music that sounded almost sweet to the tired lad. And high above his head, in the far-off sky, the stars twinkled and glowed like glittering points of fire.

"Purty little things them stars be," he said to himself; "I wonder if they be livin', an' if they're cold like me?"

For a long time he watched them; for they seemed like friendly eyes looking down upon him as he shivered there in the bitter cold, and he wondered why it was that he should be houseless, homeless, and alone, in that great city that was full of wealth as well as full of poverty.

There was no sheltering home for houseless children, or, if so, he had never heard of such a place; no society for the prevention of cruelty to boys and girls. There were hundreds of others like himself he knew, who had to shift for themselves as best they could, and live or die, just as it might happen, for nobody seemed to care.

And yet many people did care, and were saddened every day by the sight of suffering

children all about them, and sighed to themselves'
" Oh, that something could be done ! " and yet
remained helpless, because the work was so great,
and nobody led the way. Since then, among
others, a gentle lady has come to the rescue, and
has sheltered and fed many a poor perishing lad
and girl, and sent them to brighter climes beyond
the sea ; and one of Liverpool's noblest citizens has
made their cause his own, and pleaded for them in
brave and noble words in the British House of
Commons and in many another place.

But the tide of Christian charity flows all too
slowly yet, and children are perishing all about us,
with none to save.

How long Billy crouched there watching the
stars he never knew : but they began to grow dim
and to vanish at length, at least he fancied so,
while the wind wailed away in the distance and
died in the softest sighs, then all grew dusk and
still, for sweet sleep had stolen over him. And
there among the quiet dead he rested, and forgot
his care and suffering, while the pale stars looked
down upon his white upturned face, and the night
dew matted his curling locks.

It was about six o'clock in the morning when Levi Lobb, the sexton, came to the church to see that the fire was all right, for the vicar of St. Chad's was always anxious that the church should be well warmed on Christmas Day.

Levi was a short man, and looked all the shorter by reason of his excessive stoutness. Levi prided himself on being a " broad " man. His face was broad, his chest was broad, he had broad feet and broad hands. His legs stood wide apart and appeared to have no knees, his eyes were small, and like his legs, stood far apart ; his head was bald, his face clean shaved, and his mouth, being destitute of teeth, seemed to be of enormous dimensions. There could be no doubt that Levi was a " broad " man, and if his sympathies were not quite as broad as his chest, they could not be considered narrow ; while in religious matters he made it his boast that " he never quarrelled with a man as worshipped a different religion to himself."

Levi tripped lightly down the steps towards the cellar-door on the morning in question—if such a form as Levi's could ever be said to trip at all—

another moment and his broad foot would have been on little Billy Walton's chest, but fortunately for Billy—perhaps for both—he drew back in time.

" Hullo," he said to himself, feeling considerably frightened, " what 'ave we 'ere ? "

The next moment he was gently prodding Billy in the ribs with his walking stick.

" Come, young un," he said, " wake up, what yer mean by trespussin' 'ere ? "

For some seconds Billy did not stir, which led to more prodding in the ribs with a less gentle hand. At length he opened his eyes and wailed fretfully, " Don't, please, I ain't a doing no 'arm to nobody."

" Well, that's true like enough," said Levi, " but I wants to get in to see after the fire, an' ye are lyin' right across the door."

" Well, wait a minnit," said Billy, " I can't move yet I'm that stiff, this are a coldish corner to sleep in."

" Cold," said Levi, with considerable emphasis, " I wonder ye are not dead an' froze."

" I be froze," said Billy, " an' I wish I were

dead. But though I've tried 'ard to die lots o' times, I can't die for the life o' me."

"Well, get up, lad," said Levi, kindly, for his heart had been touched by Billy's words; "get up an' come in to the fire and I'll soon get yer warmed."

"Nay, I'll keep outside o' it, if you please," said Billy, scrambling to his feet.

"'Course I didn't mean to put yer inter the furniss," said Levi, somewhat taken aback.

However, without any more words the door was soon unlocked, the gas lighted, and Levi with a poker six feet long was stirring up the furnace fire till it roared again.

Billy dropped into a low wooden rocking chair which Levi had conveyed to the furnace room for his own special use and comfort. Here the old man had spent many an hour puffing deliberately at his long pipe, while the winter storms had raved and wailed outside. His wife did not allow him to smoke at home. Indeed she did not know he smoked at all; she thought she had broken him off that bad habit when she married him ten years before.

"Nay, Levi," she said, before the honeymoon was over, "my fust husband wern't allowed to smoke, an' I'm sure I'm not goin' to allow you."

Levi resisted a little at first, but he had to yield in the long run. But after that he spent considerably more time in the furnace room of St. Chad's Church than he had been in the habit of doing.

After a while Billy began to feel as though he were in paradise. The room was so cosy that he felt as though he would like to spend the remainder of the winter there.

Levi busied himself in chopping wood, breaking up coal, and other like jobs that wanted doing. When everything had been arranged, however, to his satisfaction, he came and stood in front of Billy, and placing his broad hands on his broad hips, eyed him all over.

"What's yer name ? " he said at length.

"Billy," was the answer.

"What else ? " said Levi ; "an' where d'ye live, an' what d'ye do, an' who's yer parents ? "

Billy answered all these questions without any hesitation, and to Levi's evident satisfaction.

"Well, Billy," he said at length, "I'm goin'

home to breakfast now ; an' if ye'll promise not to meddle with anything, I'll leave ye in charge till I come back again. I'm Levi Lobb, the sexton of this church ; an' I can't 'elp saying this, afore I go, that ye've had a very close squeak."

" Which way ? " said Billy.

" Why, I nearly 'ad my foot on yer coming down them steps."

" Lor ! " said Billy, a look of astonishment spreading itself over his face, and he fixed his eyes on Levi's large bulk, and seemed to measure him from head to foot.

" Well," said Levi, " what are ye a thinkin' on ? '

" I'm thinkin' I've 'ad a 'orrible escape from a narrow death," said Billy, with much seriousness.

" Billy," said Levi, looking grave, " you jumble up things considerable, an' turn 'em wrong way 'bout. I fear yer eddecation's been sadly neglected."

" Dunno," Billy answered, " don't know what that are."

" Dear me," was the reply, " I feared as much but I'll put ye through yer Catechism when I comes back."

"Is that a small place?" Billy asked, in some astonishment.

"What a small place?" asked Levi.

"The Caterkism?" said Billy.

"Why it aint no place at all," said Levi shortly. "It is the—well, it is the—the—well, blame me, it aint nothin' else, it's the Catechism, and nothing more."

"Oh!" Billy answered, trying to look wise, and the next moment Levi had gone.

"Well, he's a queer old bloke, any road," Billy said to himself, wriggling himself back into the depths of the rocking-chair, "but I reckon he's the right sort, after all."

And, with this reflection, he closed his eyes, and, under the influence of the genial warmth, was soon fast asleep.

CHAPTER VI.

"I'M SO GLAD I'VE FOUND YOU."

"She was a phantom of delight
When first she gleamed upon my sight;
A lovely apparition, sent
To be a moment's ornament;
Her eyes as stars of twilight fair,
Like twilight's, too, her dusky hair."
                              WORDSWORTH.

BILLY was still fast asleep in the rocking-chair when Levi returned, but the noise the latter made in stirring up the fire caused him to open his eyes with a start, and when Levi handed him a big square of bun-loaf, all sleepiness vanished in a moment.

"Mr. Levi," he said, "ye're a brick, tho' yer be so round."

"Ay," said Levi, looking down over his vest; "I be a queer shape brick, aint I?"

" Ay, rayther," said Billy.

" And yet," said Levi, looking serious, " I can mind the time very well when I 'ad a waist like a girl."

" You don't say so ? " said Billy, in astonishment.

" It's as true as the Catechism," said Levi.

" Lor ! " was Billy's somewhat dubious observation, and then he proceeded to devour the bun-loaf in silence.

That done, and Levi having mended the fire to his satisfaction, Billy was requested to vacate the rocking-chair, and haul up a large block of hard wood stowed away in a corner of the rambling cellar, which Levi said would make a capital seat for him.

" Where is it ? " said Billy.

" In yon corner," said Levi, pointing with his fat forefinger in the direction. " It's 'art o' oak, I reckon ; for there's no splittin' it, an' is as heavy as a stone. I'd fetch it myself, but I'm short i' th' wind an' none so good at stoopin'. But ye're strong Billy, an' a little exercise will do yer good an' loosen yer jints."

" Ken I carry it ? " asked Billy.

"Oh no," was the answer, " Ye'll 'ave to 'aul it ; but there's a nail druv in it with a piece o' cord round it.   Put the cord over yer shoulder and lay too, an' it'll come."

"All right," said Billy, and proceeded at once to carry out his instructions, while Levi stood with legs far apart to watch the performance.

To find the cord and put it over his shoulder preparatory to hauling was an easy matter.   But when Billy bent himself to the task the block would not move.

" Ye'll 'ave to give a little jerk at start," said Levi ; · " now wait till I give the signal.   One ! two ! three ! hoff."

" Ye 'ad better be hoff yerself," was the thought that flashed through Billy's mind, as with a jerk the cord snapped, and before Levi could move out of the way, Billy's head was planted in the centre of his stomach.

With a helpless look round him, and a great gasp, Levi sat down with a flop on the floor ; while Billy almost bursting with laughter fell backwards in a similar position.

For several seconds Levi gasped in a most distressing manner, and rolled his eyes round the room as though in mute appeal for assistance.

"Billy," he said at length between his gasps, "this is serious."

"Ay," said Billy, looking grave; "it are, but it might ha' been wuss."

"Worse, Billy?" Levi exclaimed.

"Ay," said Billy, "I might ha' run agin the wall, an' knocked my brains out."

"But what of *me*?" Levi asked, helplessly.

"Well you are soft, Levi," said Billy; "werry soft."

"Billy!" said Levi, looking very stern; "if there's one thing I can't stand it's being hit in the wind."

"No!" said Billy, innocently; "but yer 'adn't far to sit, that's a mussy."

"You think so," said Levi, severely.

"And there wern't nothin' to 'urt," went on Billy. "I know'd a chap once, as sat down all of a flop on the wrong end o' a tin-tack, but he didn't sit there very long."

"No?" said Levi, looking interested.

"No, he got up pretty quick, an' he talked

so 'ard that everybody 'ad to get out o' his reach."

"I've no breath to talk 'ard," said Levi, struggling to his feet, "an' besides twern't your fault; but I'll not be able to put you through your Catechism to-day."

"Oh, never mind that," Billy answered.

"But ye must go to church instead," said Levi. I'll put yer in a snug co'ner behin' the door curtins. Are ye fond o' music?"

"Oh, ay. I knowed a chap as could play the 'cordial bootiful, but I likes the music best as turns with a 'andel."

"Humph," said Levi, dropping into his chair. "I fear, boy, ye've spoiled my dinner, an' hupset me for the day."

"I'm werry sorry," said Billy, who, however, was highly pleased at the same time that the old man took the affair so kindly.

A few minutes before service commenced, and while Levi was busy tolling the bell, Billy crept into the corner behind the curtains, that had been pointed out to him. He had never been inside a church before, and so was greatly impressed by its size and splendour. But when the organ began, the music drove everything else out of his mind.

" Lor," he grunted to himself, " that licks the 'cordial out o' sight."

There were not a great many people in the church, so that the voice of the minister echoed somewhat mournfully through the place. When, however, he got into the pulpit, and announced his text, Billy was all eagerness and anticipation.

" And thou, Bethlehem Ephratah, though thou be little among the thousands of Judah, yet out of thee shall He come forth unto me that is to be ruler in Israel, whose goings forth have been from of old, from everlasting," were the words that he read out of the big Bible, but, alas! they were an unknown tongue to Billy. And the sermon was equally above his head. Such words as atonement, substitution, justification, regeneration, sacrifice, and propitiation, were of frequent occurrence, but they were meaningless sounds to him, and almost so to Cricket, who was in the church with her little brother Jack in her arms.

Billy was greatly disappointed, for Levi had told him if he listened attentively he would hear some-

G

thing good. The singing and the prayers he had enjoyed, for they touched his heart strangely, though he could not interpret their meaning. But the sermon was not for him. No word of it touched his need or came home to his heart. The high sounding phrases were for the rich and learned ; the ignorant and poor listened in vain.

Billy was fast asleep before the sermon was half through, for he was always ready for a nap when he got into a comfortable corner ; and until this morning such corners had been scarce.

He was wide awake again, however, during the singing of the last hymn, and from his corner, unobserved, he watched the people rise slowly from their seats, and file quietly out of the church.

At last he caught sight of Cricket, but could scarcely believe his own eyes. "Golly!" he exclaimed, in his excitement, "it's her, by jabbers, it are ! *Hi, Cricket !* " he called out quite loudly ; and then, seeing the people start and stare round the church, he drew quickly back among the curtains.

"My stars, it's her," he muttered to himself; " nobody never 'ad heyes like her afore."

Cricket had recognised his voice in a moment, and loitered behind to speak to him, and when everybody had got out of the church, she walked close up to the curtains, and called softly, "Billy."

"I know'd it were you, Cricket," he said, pushing out his head.

"Oh, I'm so glad I've found you," said Cricket, and there was gladness in the sound of her voice, and in the light in her eyes.

"An' I'm glad too," Billy answered, coming hastily out of his corner.

"And now," said Cricket, "I want you to come with me."

This was an invitation that did not require to be repeated, and the next minute they were walking away together in the direction of Cooper's Row.

"Father's come home," said Cricket, ere they had gone many steps. "He's been let out on bail; I don't know what that is exactly; anyhow, he's home, an' is cooking the dinner; an' he said he'd be glad for me an' Jack to go to church, to be out of the way. He *was* pleased when he found the goose all right; an' when I told him how you'd brought it, he said you were a trump, and if I saw you anywhere, I was to ask you home to dinner."

"Did he say that?" asked Billy, in astonishment.

"Ay; he's real kind sometimes, specially if he's pleased; so let's hurry on. Likely dinner 'll be quite ready when we get there, for father's a capital cook."

True enough the dinner was quite ready, and such a dinner as Billy had never seen before. He declared the smell of it nearly took his breath away, and was so good that one ought to have a piece of bread to eat with it.

But good as the smell was, the taste was better still, so good indeed that Billy was in great danger of making himself ill.

At length he laid down his knife and fork in despair.

"It aint no use," he said, "I never was licked afore in the eatin' line, but I'm licked this time."

Richard Chase laughed in his heavy fashion, but he said very little to Billy and scarcely more to Cricket.

He had greatly changed since he came to Liverpool. His mates declared that he was a hundred times more spry and 'cute than when he came, and there was some truth in their remark. The heavy stolid look had passed away from his face, but there had come into his eyes a look of cunning and suspicion, and around his mouth was a set expression of recklessness and defiance. He was "sharper" in manner truly: but his moral sense had become more and more dulled and blunted. He never had been overburdened with what is termed "proper pride" or self-respect, and what little he had remaining had been crushed out by the events of the previous night. It had always been a boast of his that "he had never been locked up."

But he could boast of it no longer. He had seen the inside of a police station, and had spent a night there, and on the morrow he would have to appear before the magistrate and submit to a fine. He did not expect anything worse than that.

But the very fact of having been "locked up," was sufficient to make him utterly reckless. What did it matter. It's as well to be hanged for a sheep as for a lamb. A hundred times in the police station or *once*, was all the same. Such were his reflections.

And with this feeling of recklessness and defiance he started out soon after dinner to join his mates at the " Royal George."

Cricket settled herself down to have a long chat with Billy, who was to her as yet an unsolved problem. She had never met with a lad that had so interested her. He was such a mixture of cunning and simplicity, of ignorance and strong common sense ; of superstition and scepticism, that she was at a loss how to gauge him.

Being Christmas Day—and finding that Billy was ignorant as to its meaning—she told him all the Gospel story as well as she could remember it.

Billy listened very attentively till she had finished, and then remarked—" Well, Cricket, it aint a bad yarn on the 'ole. But if ye'll listen, I'll tell yer a heap better tale nor that, an' one that's true too."

" True, Billy," said Cricket in astonishment. " Do you think what I told you aint true ? "

" In course it aint true," said Billy with a laugh. "Yer didn't think ye were going to catch this bird with chaff, did yer. Oh, Cricket, I didn't think ye thought I were so simple as that."

"Oh, Billy!" was all that Cricket could say. But there was inexpressible sadness in her tone.

"Now yer needn't put on in that way," said Billy, feeling somewhat puzzled. "An' parts o' yer story may be true p'raps, but that about dying for those who spit on Him, and abused Him, that are a trifle too much to swaller, an' that 'bout coming to life again. In course, Cricket, yer don't swaller that?"

"But I do," said Cricket, "for it's quite true."

"Well, then, all as I can say is," said Billy, "that I didn't think as ye were so simple."

This reply silenced Cricket for a while, but she was not discouraged. She was sure Billy was not a bad boy, notwithstanding all he said. He was truthful, she knew, though he would not believe the truth; and honest in heart, though not always in action.

For a while no other word was spoken, and Cricket laid little Jack in the cradle and set to work to mend the fire, for the cold had increased as the afternoon wore on, and the snow had begun to come down in sober earnest.

When Cricket spoke again she said, " Look here, Billy, you must go to church again, an' to the ragged school, an' ye'll get told lots of things that you don't know, an' learn how to be good."

" Do you go ? " said Billy.

" Ay, whenever I can," was the answer.

" Oh then I'll go too," he said. " I'll go any-wheres wi' you, Cricket. But hark 'ow the wind is a wailin' in the chimbley an' see 'ow the snow is a pepperin' down, aint this scrumpshus that I aint to go 'bout in it. P'raps yer faather 'd let me stay all night ? "

" Oh yes, I think he will," said Cricket, and then there was silence again, save for the snow beating on the window panes, and the moaning of the wind in the chimney.

About half-past eleven Richard Chase returned, drunk and angry.

" What, you 'ere still, you lazy young vaga-bond," he said to Billy. The next moment he had caught him by the collar of his ragged jacket and had flung him into the street.

"Oh, father!" exclaimed Cricket.

But he turned upon her savagely. "You clear off to bed," he said, "you an' the brat, or I'll fling you after him."

Cricket knew better than to answer him back while he was in his present mood, and catching up little Jack in her arms she rushed up the stairs.

Many hours passed away however before she fell asleep. How could she sleep with that bitter night wind wailing and moaning round the house, and the cruel snow like fine hail beating against the windows all the night, and knowing that little Billy Walton, without a home, without a friend, was out in the wintry streets suffering, perhaps dying, in the snow.

CHAPTER VII.

"IT WAS A COLD CORNER AT BEST."

> " What now is left me, but to raise
> From thee, lorn spot, my spirit's gaze,
> To lift through tears my straining eye,
> Up to my Father's house on high?"·
>
> HEMANS.

BILLY Walton had the happy knack of generally alighting on his feet. Moreover, he was not often discouraged at small difficulties, and was, as a rule, quite disposed to look at the bright side of things, and make the best of a bad bargain. Hence, when he found himself on his feet in the middle of "Cooper's Row" he was by no means in despair. He had been in as bad a plight before, and ·most likely would be again. So the only thing for him to do was to "keep a stiff upper-lip," as he termed it, and search for a dry corner somewhere.

It is true that his sudden ejection from the warm room to the cold street did not by any means improve his temper; and for several seconds he executed a kind of war-dance in the snow in the front of No. 13, and wound up the performance by sundry flourishes of his fists, as a kind of challenge to his invisible foe.

After this little performance, he seemed somewhat easier in his mind, and started out in search of a place of shelter, not by any means an easy task in the present state of the weather. Beneath his bare feet the snow crunched as he passed swiftly along, and all around him the flakes swirled and danced, and found their way through his tattered raiment to his bare skin. He was ready to cry with cold ere he had gone many yards, but he resolutely set his teeth together, and clenched his little fists in defiance.

Naturally, he followed the route of the previous night, but found that the narrow passage down to the cellar door was half full of snow, and so afforded him no protection at all.

He now began to blame himself for going off with Cricket without first telling Levi where he was going ; for somehow he had the idea that the old man had taken a liking to him, and meant to be his friend. And in this surmise he was not far wrong. Not that Levi was altogether disinterested in his desire to help Billy ; he saw—or fancied he saw—a chance of benefiting himself at the same time. He had long felt the need of a little help in dusting the church and keeping it clean.

Some of the work required a good deal of stooping, and some of the corners were so narrow that he could hardly get into them at all. And many times he wished that he had a quick handy lad or girl of his own. Hence in Billy he saw just what he wanted. The lad was quick, suitable, and had all his wits about him, and very likely, for an odd meal or two, or a few coppers, he would be glad to help him on a Saturday in dusting the church.

He had intended making Billy the offer after the service on Christmas morning, especially as there was only one clear day between Christmas and Sunday, and that day was certain to be a specially busy one. He was, therefore, considerably disappointed when he discovered that Billy was nowhere to be found.

During the afternoon and evening he returned several times for the purpose of seeing that the fire was all right (for the vicar had impressed upon him the necessity of "keeping the heat well up" till Sunday), and each time he had expected to find Billy loitering about, or, at least, of stumbling across his footprints, and each time he had returned disappointed.

"Blame me," he said to himself, as he banked up the fire with slack, and prepared to take his departure for the night. "I don't know why I should worrit about the boy ; he aint nothin' to me, an' there's plenty o' other starvin' an' 'ouseless brats in Liverpool, so let 'im take his chance."

Yet, notwithstanding this reflection, Levi did worrit. Billy had touched the old man's heart in a way he could not account for. He had seen ragged and destitute children before, and had been teased by some of them almost beyond endurance ; but somehow this lad had appealed to his sympathies in a way that none of the others had done. He had found him asleep in the silent churchyard, with his pale face upturned to the stars, and almost frozen to death. He had warmed him back to life

again by " his own " furnace fire ; had fed him with
food taken without his wife's consent or knowledge ; he had even been knocked down by him—
and Levi smiled all over his broad face at the re-
membrance of the morning's adventure. " Blame
me," he chuckled, " he's a most amoosin' little dog,
an' there aint no gammon 'bout him either. I wish
I were sartin the little chap had shelter this snowy
night."

On the top of the steps Levi waited several
seconds in the swirling snow, as if undecided what
to do.

" It aint no use," he grunted at length ; "I'll be
froze myself if I stay 'ere much longer," and with a
hasty glance from side to side, he started for his
home.

Scarcely more than half an hour later Billy stood
with his bare feet on the same spot, and looked
down the opening towards the cellar door with
a feeling akin to despair; his teeth were chattering, his hands and face were blue with cold.
Oh, how much more blessed the dead sleeping
under their coverlet of snow than he ! They felt
no cold, they knew no hunger nor want ; their

troubles were over, and their hearts still for ever.

So Billy thought, as with a great sigh that was almost a sob, he turned quickly away to continue his search for a place of shelter. Along the south side of the church he carefully picked his way till he reached a large porch that was blocked by a large iron gate swung across its entire width. The porch was Gothic, the gate was square, hence there was a large triangular opening at the top.

" Jabbers ! " said Billy, with chattering teeth, " if I could on'y climb over that gate I'd be in clover," though what clover meant he had not, poor boy, the remotest idea.

For some time he stood before the gate in evident indecision. " I've a good mind to tackle it," he said to himself, " for the wind's t'other side of the church, an' I'd be nice an' sheltered if I could on'y get in."

With Billy to think was often to act, indeed he often acted without thinking at all. So without any further hesitation, he bent his energies to the task of climbing over the gate. The exercise was on the whole profitable, for it brought into play all his muscles, and warmed him as nothing else just then would have done.

"Jabbers!" he said, as he tried different methods of getting over the top without being impaled, "this are a ticklish bis'ness an' no mistake."

But Billy was not to be defeated if he could help it, and at length, after what seemed an interminable period, he found himself on the right side of the gate. To drop to the ground was his only care, but this was not so easy as he had imagined it would be, for instead of reaching the floor when he loosened his hands and fell from the gate, he found himself unconsciously turning a somersault, and the next moment he found himself suspended, with his head where his heels should have been.

"Murder an' bees-wax!" he ejaculated, "this are a caution an' no mistake. I'm hanged at last, an' wrong hend up."

For a moment or two Billy remained passive, for the purpose of reflection. Then he commenced pawing round in an aimless kind of fashion, but grasping one of the bars of the gate at length he was able to drag himself up into a horizontal position.

"Now, Billy," he said to himself, "you mun' strip for this bis'ness," and, with a dexterous movement, he slipped first one arm out of his jacket and then another, and so dropped lightly to the ground. To climb the gate again and release his jacket was a very small matter.

Billy was quite warm by this time, and in great good humour with himself and with everybody else. How he should get out again was a matter that did not trouble him in the least; if he could get in, in the dark, he would surely be able to get out in the daylight, so he let to-morrow care for itself, and tried to make himself comfortable for the present.

It will be readily imagined, however, that a church porch, with no protection from the wind and snow but an iron gate, is not the most desirable place in which to spend a winter's night, a fact which Billy was not slow in discovering.

Fortunately, there was a large "sunk" mat lying in front of the door, the whole width of the porch; this indeed was the only redeeming feature about the place. Billy got underneath it at first, but found the floor so damp and cold that he was glad to try some other plan. At length, after immense difficulty, he managed to roll the mat quite round him, and here he remained for the night like a rabbit in a hole.

It was better than being out in the snow, but it was a cold corner at best. He tried hard to sleep, but found the cold so intense after a while, that that became altogether out of the question. Besides, his limbs got cramped by the peculiar posture he had to assume, and altogether the night was as comfortless as anything he had ever known.

Around the gables of the church the wind moaned and wailed, as though evil spirits were holding carnival in the churchyard ; and through the iron gate the snow was drifted more and more, and danced in the chill air of the porch in wildest revel.

Poor little Billy could not help wondering, as his teeth chattered in the bitter cold, whether the rich and great in their fine houses and beds of down, ever gave a thought to the homeless suffering children who were dying in the streets.

It seemed to him a very selfish, cruel world, as far as he could see. It was every one for himself,

and those who could not care for themselves must
droop and die. How little would make him com‹
fortable, and even happy; how many could give
him that little and be none the poorer. And yet
here he was, this winter's night, homeless, destitute,
forsaken!

He had never heard of God, except as a name
to swear by. Never heard of Providence, had
never been taught to pray; and so he knew of no
one to whom he might look for help, nor realised
in his loneliness and pain that God was near.

CHAPTER VIII.

"'PERHAPS HE'S FROZE IN THE SNOW,' SHE SAID."

"What is noble?—to inherit
    Wealth, estate, and proud degree?
There must be some other merit
    Higher yet than these for me!
Something greater far must enter
    Into life's majestic span,
Fitted to create and centre
    True nobility in man."

SWAIN.

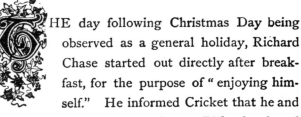HE day following Christmas Day being observed as a general holiday, Richard Chase started out directly after breakfast, for the purpose of "enjoying himself." He informed Cricket that he and some of his mates were going to Birkenhead, and that he would not be back again till evening. Cricket knew very well what that meant, and her heart sank at the news. Still for little Jack's sake she tried to keep up her spirits and hope for the best.

Outside the snow lay white and deep, with scarcely a track upon it as yet in the middle of the court, while the great city all around seemed as if asleep, so muffled was every sound by the thick carpet of snow. Cricket could not help wondering what had become of little Billy Walton. It seemed such a cruel thing to fling the poor lad, like a dog, into the streets on such a wintry night, and she wondered if her father had any recollection of what he had done. He made no allusion to the matter, however, and after he had gone out, Cricket made up a good fire in the hope that Billy would find his way back to the room from which he had been so rudely expelled.

Hour after hour passed away, however, and Cricket watched and waited in vain for his coming. For a full hour she kept dinner waiting—the remains of yesterday's goose—in the hope that Billy would make his appearance. But when one o'clock had passed, and two, and three, and the short afternoon began to fade in darkness, and still he showed no sign of coming, she began to fear that some evil had befallen him.

" Perhaps he's froze in the snow," she said to

herself, and the tears started to her eyes at the thought. Her friends, even her acquaintances, were so few that to lose one of them seemed to make an enormous gap in her life. And though she had never seen Billy until two days ago, it seemed to her as if she had known him for months. They had become acquainted in such a curious fashion, and he had told her so much of his life, that she felt that while they lived they could never again be strangers to each other. Hence, if Billy were dead it would be like losing an old friend.

They had been in Liverpool now more than two months, but she felt almost as much a stranger in it as when they came. Often she had longed to go and see some of its wonderful sights, but had never been able to find the time, or even had she the time, she had no one to guide her, and she had all a country child's fear of missing her way and getting lost in the wilderness of streets.

Within a radius of a quarter of a mile from Cooper's Row she felt on familiar ground, but all beyond that was an unknown and an unexplored country to her.

"Perhaps, when summer comes, I'll be able to go and see the great Hall an' the Monument an' all the other fine places I've heard so much about," she said to herself. "An' oh, I should like to sail on the big river once more, an' see the fine ships, and the shining water, an' a bit of the blue mountains far away."

Poor child, she had all her mother's love and enthusiasm for the beauties of Nature, and she never thought of the mountains without thinking also of Brook Cottage, and the singing beck, and the big hawthorn, and the quiet fields all around.

It all came back to her again this wintry afternoon as she sat in the waning light, with her hands lying listlessly in her lap, and her eyes fixed on the fire. But she did not see the fire, she was looking through it and beyond it, and before her mental vision was a beautiful picture of green fields steeped in summer's sunshine, and beyond the fields broken and wooded country all clad in living green, and beyond the woods the blue Welsh mountains rising up to the sky, and in her ears were the music of the brook and the sweeter music of her mother's voice.

How long she might have remained there dreaming her dreams of bygone days, it is impossible to say, had they not been suddenly interrupted by a timid knock at the door, which made Cricket spring out of her chair with a start and rush to open the door.

Before she could do so, however, the door was thrown open, and Billy Walton stood before her, but so changed that Cricket scarcely recognised him.

"Don't yer know me, Cricket?" said Billy, grinning all over his face.

"Oh yes, I know you now," said Cricket, "but I hardly knew you at first; but come up to the fire, and let me look at you. I am so glad you've come; I've been expectin' you all day."

"'Ave yer?" said Billy, his eyes sparkling with pleasure; "I'm glad o' that."

"But where did you get your clothes an' your cap, Billy? You do look funny."

"Does I?" said Billy, warming his hands in front of the fire; "but that's just what I've come to tell yer 'bout: I'm in luck's way, Cricket, an' I b'leeve I've made my fortin'," and he put his hand into his pocket and pulled out four coppers; "now look at that, Cricket, an' then say if I aint rich for once in my life."

"Well," said Cricket, opening her eyes in astonishment, "you are well off, Billy; but how did it all come about?"

"Well," said Billy, with an air of importance, "you knows Levi, don't yer?"

"No," said Cricket, "I don't think I do."

"What, not know that rolly-polly chap as keeps the church warm, an' pulls the bell-rope?"

"Oh yes, I know him," said Cricket, "but I didn't know as his name were Levi."

"Well, it are," said Billy. "Levi Lobb, that's his name; an' he's a real brick. He foun' me this mornin' in the porch o' the church where I went last night, ter get out o' the snow. I were near froze, he said, an' within a hace o' kingdom come. But, lor', he warmed me up in no time, an' gived me sich a breakfas' as never was. An' then he goes off to the vicar—that's the chap, you know, as talks so much wot nobody knows nothin' 'bout in the church—well, he goes to the vicar, wot 'as a lot o' boys, an' begs these 'ere togs for me.

Splendashus, aint it ?   Lor', I feels just like a new one.   An' that aint ole, either."

"Not all ? " said Cricket, in some surprise.

"No !" said Billy, pushing his hands into his pockets and drawing himself up to his full height, " I've got a sitivation."

" A situation, Billy ? "

" A sitivation, Cricket ?   I'm to 'ave four coppers a week, wi' a lot o' wittels to boot : to say nothin' o' lodgins, when the fire's on ; but that's a secret atween Levi an' me."

" But what will you have to do ? " asked Cricket.

" Oh, I'm to 'elp Levi," said Billy.   " He's got too big to get inter small co'ners ; he's werry round, is Levi : werry !   But 'e's a brick for all that ; an' I'm to dust the box as the vicar stands in, an' the benches the folks sits on, an' a lot o' hodds and hends, too numerous to mention."

" Well, I'm very glad," said Cricket, reflectively.

" Ay," said Billy, with quite an air of importance, " bringin' of that bird 'ere were quite a stroke of luck, though I were terrible mad at you for 'spectin' I would steal anything from you, but it were a good thing.   I jist went straight from 'ere to the church, an' dropped asleep agin the cellar door. There Levi found me, an' we got quite frien'ly. I b'leeve, Cricket, my fortin's made."

"Very likely it is," Cricket answered, "that is, Billy, if you are careful, and don't tell no lies, and never take anything that don't belong to you."

"Well, I b'leeve working on that tack 'll pay best," Billy answered, after a pause. "Any road, I'm goin' to try that dodge for a bit, an' see 'ow it 'll hanser. An' I'm goin' to church again to-morrer, and to the ragged skule in the afternoon."

"Oh, that is right, Billy!" Cricket answered, a glad smile overspreading her face.

'Oh, ay," Billy answered, "when yer told me you were goin' the thing were settled; an' so I promised Levi right off, when he axed me. Lor, he smiled from ear to ear, just like a frog might do; for he thought I done it jist to please 'im."

"Well, I hope you did it to please him as well as me," said Cricket.

"No, I didn't," said Billy. "Yer told me I mustn't tell no lies, an' I aint agoin' to begin now."

To this Cricket made no reply, for the simple reason that she had no reply to make.

After tea they talked about many things, and Billy promised Cricket that when the fine weather came he would take her to see St. George's Hall, and the Town Hall, and the Custom House, and the Docks, and all the other sights of Liverpool. And, what was even more inviting still to Cricket, he promised to show her the way to the top of Everton Brow, from which spot they would be able to see right across the river, and catch a glimpse of the blue mountains of Wales away in the distance.

At a prospect like this Cricket opened all her heart to Billy, and told him about her early home in the quiet country, and of Cefn Lee, her mother's home, away behind the glorious hills, and of the longing she had ever since she could remember, to explore that fairyland—to her—where her grandparents lived, and see the old people whose praises her mother so often sang.

" Oh well," said Billy, as he rose to go, " we'll go there, Cricket, some day ; see if we don't."

That night Billy slept in Levi's rocking-chair in front of the furnace fire, and the next morning— being now tolerably respectably dressed—he sat in the same pew with Cricket and little Jack.

His experience in the ragged school, however, was not soon forgotten, either by himself or his teacher. Being by no means shy, and quick-witted to boot, he plied the young lady who presided over the class in which he found himself with questions which she found impossible to answer, and finished up by declaring that, though she were pretty good at spinning a yarn, he could cap any of the tales she had told, and vouch for the truth of them into the bargain.

He did not use those words, but there could be no mistake about his meaning. The young lady in question, as may readily be supposed, was greatly shocked ; and tried her best to awaken in Billy a more reverential and less sceptical spirit, but with no very great success.

Billy was by nature incredulous ; moreover, his training, or no training, had directly tended to make him suspicious and mistrustful of everything and everybody. Billy's principle was, never to take anything on trust if he could possibly help it. He had found the world—or that part of it into which he had been thrown—so false and deceitful, that he naturally supposed that nobody was honest except under compulsion, and that nobody told the truth if the end could be more easily gained by telling lies.

Hence, when his teacher looked grave, and tried to impress upon him that what she had been saying was serious and sober truth, Billy glanced at her good-humouredly out of the corners of his eyes, and completely upset her gravity by saying, " He guessed she were a hold hand, and pretty used to tellin' stretchers."

Yet he was so evidently sincere, and so respectful withal, that she could not be offended with him. His was a case that would undoubtedly tax all her powers, but she was resolved to do her best. There was such a clear, steadfast light in his eyes, and such an honest ring in his voice, that she was quite satisfied that the lad's heart was right, and that in the long run he would well repay all the trouble bestowed upon him.

Billy told Cricket that he liked going to school "fust class," and said that he should go on week-nights as well, whenever he had the chance, so that he might learn to write as well as read.

CHAPTER IX.

"IT'S BEING GOOD."

" Ambition, pride, revenge, depart,
    And folly flies her chastening rod ;
  She makes the humble, contrite heart,
    A temple of the living God."

MONTGOMERY.

URING the next few months both
Cricket and Billy learnt many things
and passed through many experiences.
Under the combined influence of Levi,
Cricket, and Miss Bute (the teacher at
the Ragged School), Billy may be said to have
turned over a new leaf. Indeed, to the poor homeless, friendless lad the whole aspect of the world
was changed. He was never now without a copper
to pay for a night's lodging, and never a day passed
but he got at least one substantial meal.

Each Saturday he helped Levi to dust the

church ; and while the cold weather lasted, and the church needed warming, he was allowed to spend two, and sometimes three, nights a week before the furnace fire ; but this was a secret known only to Levi and himself.

During the many hours they were thus thrown together, Levi seized the opportunity of putting Billy through the Catechism, and of explaining many matters which he considered Billy was sadly ignorant of. It cannot be said, however, that Billy was very much the wiser for Levi's instructions, though he listened very attentively, and was careful not to cross his benefactor if he could possibly help it. On the other hand, however, he sorely puzzled Levi sometimes by the questions he asked him.

One evening while seated before the fire, at the close of the evening service, Billy rather astonished Levi by saying "he could not make head nor tail of none o' it."

" What, Billy," said Levi, aghast, "an' arter all my teachin' too ? "

" Well, I guess," said Billy, "I've got a mighty thick yed, an' there aint no gettin' no sense inter it."

"I'm afear'd so," said Levi, pulling deliberately at his pipe, "but what is it that's bogglin' yer pertickler?"

"Well," said Billy, slowly, "yer keeps talkin' 'bout religion, an' the good o' it, an' the duty o' goin' to church, an' all that, but though I've been listenin' all day wi' all the eyes I've got in my yed, I'll be roasted if I ken make out wot it's all about."

Levi pulled out his pipe at this and looked hard at Billy for several seconds without speaking; then drawing a long breath, he said :—

"Billy, we mustn't expect to know everythink 'ere, 'an lots o' things are beyond knowin' altogether. Besides, religion's a very ticklish question, because there's so many sorts o' it, an' it takes a very cute man to know 'em all, an' which are right sorts an' which aint. Now our religion at St. Chad's is this :—Go to church reg'lar, say the Litany, prayers, 'Postles' Creed, an' them things at the proper times, turn yer faces to the east at the right place, bow yer heads at the name o' the Saviour, an' allers say grace at meal times. Well, then the Catholics hev a different sort o' religion,

I'm told. They hev it in a furren langwidge; they wears long necklaces, an' counts the beads instead o' saying grace, an' they hoist up big crosses, and marches round the church a good deal, but I don't understand it fully. Then there's the Dissenters, who, our vicar says, is altogether mistook; they don't hev none of them things sca'ce, no Litany nor 'Postles' Creed, nor Ten Commandments; but they sing a goodish bit, do a lot o' talkin' an' shout amazin' in some places. Then there's lots o' other sorts o' religion; but ye'll never be able to understand it all, Billy."

"Ay! but," said Billy, "wot's the use o' it all? wot's the use o' your religion, Levi?"

"Well, as for that," said Levi, somewhat staggered, "yer bound to hev some sort o' religion you know, to please Him who is up in the sky, an' as made us all. Unless yer do the thing proper He'll not let yer come into heaven when you die."

"Oh, that's the game, is it?" said Billy, and relapsed into silence.

He was thinking over these things on the following Saturday, while busy dusting the pulpit.

Under the book-board was a thermometer, which the vicar had hung there for his own special use.

"Hullo," said Billy, holding it up into the light that he might have a better look at it. "Wot in the name o' the Ten Commandments now are this for?" and he marched off with it to Levi, who was at the other end of the church.

"Levi," he said, "wot's the name o' this little thing, 'an wot's the use of it?"

"Oh, that," said Levi, looking wise, and speaking slowly, "is a termometer."

"But wot's it for?" persisted Billy.

"Well, to tell you the truth," said Levi, dropping his voice almost to a whisper, "it's a fad of the vicar's. He thinks as it warms the pulpit, but 'atween you 'an me, Billy, I believe he might 'ave a church full on 'em, an' the church wouldn't be a bit no warmer."

"Any road," said Billy, "I'll slip this one in my pocket a bit, an' see if it warms me."

And Billy marched away with the thermometer in his pocket. He was back again, however, in less than half an hour.

" Look 'ere, Levi," he said, " ye're a pokin' fun at me."

" Nay, lad, I'm not," said Levi. " I told yer I'd no faith in them things for warmin' purposes."

"Why, the thing are as cold as a frog," said Billy. " There aint as much fire in it as in a slate pencil."

" That's what I've always said," Levi answered, "but lor, it won't do to cross the vicar; he's a mighty wise man, an' he will 'ave it hung up in the pulpit, an' he looks at it every time as he goes in, an' I just smiles to myself, an' says nothin'."

For a moment Billy looked staggered, then he marched back again to the pulpit, muttering to himself, " The vicar may be werry wise, but, accordin' to my thinkin', he don't kno' very much."

And after that day, for many a long month, Billy's faith in the vicar was considerably shaken, and he listened to his sermons with much less interest than before. A man who could believe that a little glass tube stuck on to a piece of wood would warm a pulpit, was, according to Billy's opinion, a fit subject for a lunatic asylum, and not to be taken seriously under any circumstances. It never occurred to Billy at that time, nor for long after, that Levi might be wrong in his explanations. To him Levi was a kind of walking dictionary. He seemed to know everything. Indeed, Billy was not at all certain whether it was not the immense amount of knowledge he possessed that made him so stout. How could a man be thin when he was stuffed so full of information? The only thing he wondered at was Levi's modesty in the matter. Outside the cellar the old man never boasted of his attainments, and in the presence of the vicar was all deference and humility; but this only increased Billy's respect for him. A man so simple, and yet so wise, so playful, and yet so grave, so modest, and yet crammed so full of information, caught his fancy amazingly; and so, as time went on, there was no one to whose judgment he would so soon defer as to Levi's.

In after years he came to see things in a very different light, and was at length forced to the conclusion that Levi knew just as much about religion as he did about thermometers. Yet this in no wise lessened his respect for the old man. Levi had befriended him when most in need, and never was there a period in his life after that day when he would not willingly have shared his last crust with the kindly old sexton.

But at the time to which we refer, Levi's opinion always stood first, next in order came Cricket's, and then Miss Bute's, the teacher at the Ragged School.

" Cricket," said Billy one day to her, in the early spring, as he was taking her to see some of the sights of Liverpool, " does yer know wot religion are ? "

" Ay, Billy, I think I do," she answered.

" Wot are it, then ? "

" Don't say, what are it, Billy ; say, what *is* it."

" All right, Cricket ; I allers gives in to the ladies. Wot *is* it, then ? "

" Well," said Cricket, slowly, " it's bein' good."

" Bein' fiddlesticks," said Billy, with a toss of his head. " I know'd ye weren't up to it, Cricket. You should get Levi to put yer through yer Catechism, an' then ye'd know a thing or two."

But though Cricket made no reply to this, that little sentence of hers, " It's being good," stuck in Billy's memory and refused to be dislodged. A dozen times at least that day he repeated softly to himself, " It's being good," and when he lay down to sleep that night on a heap of dirty straw, for which privilege he paid a penny, the words haunted him still, and even stole into his dreams after sleep had sealed his eyelids.

He did not allude to the matter again until many weeks later. It was a clear sunshiny afternoon in the early part of July, and they were seated on some steps not far from Everton church, looking away across the river at the green hills of Cheshire stretching away in the distance.

" It's werry bootiful, ain't it, Cricket ? " Billy said.

" Ay, Billy," she answered ; " it's like home."

" That is yer 'ome as was afore you comed to Cooper's Row ? " he asked.

" Yes," she said, her eyes filling, " the home where mother died."

" Was it yer mother as told you that religion were bein' good ? " he asked, after a pause.

" Ay," she answered, simply ; " she told me nearly all I know that is worth knowin'."

" Well, it's likely she weren't far wrong," said

Billy, reflectively, and then silence dropped down between them.

Cricket was in no mood for conversation this afternoon. The sight of the beautiful country, with the blue line of the Welsh hills in the distance had awakened a thousand memories of earlier and happier days, and aroused a hunger in her heart that nothing could appease.

Life at Cooper's Row was becoming more cheerless and desolate day by day. Even the sunshine that brightened everything else, only tended to bring out into bolder relief the squalor, and dirt, and degradation of the neighbourhood in which she lived, and to reveal more clearly the poverty of her own home.

She did her best to keep the house neat and clean, but she was almost out of heart with it, for her father begrudged every penny that was not spent in food and drink. Indeed, the drink cost so much in these days that food was often scarce in the cupboard, and little Jack had more than once cried himself to sleep of late, because there was no milk in the house and no money to purchase any.

Besides this, their clothes were sadly the worse for wear, and she had no means, poor child, of purchasing new. For the first few months after they came to Cooper's Row, Mrs. Tipple had often lent her a helping hand, but with the New Year she and her husband had betaken themselves to a more savoury neighbourhood, and Cricket was left without any help at all.

She felt the loss of Mrs. Tipple's help very keenly, but she did not give way to despair, though she was sorely tempted to do so sometimes, especially when her farther complained that his victuals were not properly cooked, and that there was not a bit of comfort in the house.

" I do my best, father," she said to him one day; " and I could do better if you'd let me have more money."

For a moment his brow clouded with anger. But the answer when it came was more kindly than she expected.

" P'raps you do," he said; " yer only a gal, the place sadly wants a woman to keep it in shape I'll have to get wed again, I expect," and without waiting for her to reply he strode out of the house.

This happened many weeks ago, and as her father had never alluded to the matter again, she was beginning to hope that his words had no meaning, and that they were only spoken to frighten her.

Still her heart was very heavy in spite of the sunshine, and the beautiful country beyond the shining river. Try as she would to hope for the best, there were moments when the memory of her father's words would shoot through her heart with a stab of pain.

She always tried to put away the thought as often as it came. It was too horrible to think about. She cherished her mother's memory with a reverence that almost amounted to worship, and the thought of anyone else coming to fill her place was too painful to be endured. At such moments she always gave little Jack an extra squeeze and an extra kiss, and the child would smile back upon her as though he knew what it meant.

They remained up on the hill-top until the sun went down behind the far-off mountains, and the chill, as well as the shadows of evening began to creep over them.

"We'll go there, some day, Cricket," Billy said, in answer to the long-drawn sigh that Cricket gave as she turned away her gaze from the mountains and prepared to descend the hill.

But she made no reply, and Billy felt rather disappointed as he sought his couch of straw, that what he had anticipated giving Cricket so much pleasure had only—to all appearance—given her pain.

CHAPTER X.

" HE WAS TERRIBLY HUMILIATED."

> " Enjoy the spring of love and youth,
>   To some good angel leave the rest ;
> For time will teach thee soon the truth—
>   There are no birds in last year's nest."
>   LONGFELLOW.

FTER that bright July afternoon recorded in the last chapter, matters began to mend a little at No. 13, Cooper's Row. A sudden revival of trade gave Richard Chase the opportunity of working overtime, which he readily availed himself of. Cricket was the first to reap the benefit of this. Working overtime meant more wages, and less time to spend it in ; less drink meant more home comforts, with an increase of kindness and good temper. And as Richard Chase made no further allusion to the matter that had troubled Cricket so, the spirits of the latter visibly revived, and she began to feel as though they were at the beginning of brighter and better days.

So the weeks slipped away till September came. Little Jack was now more than a year old, and was just beginning to toddle about the house, by the aid of table and chairs. He was a wonderfully good-tempered child, though scarcely so strong and well developed as his earlier days gave promise of. Foul air and skimmed milk were scarcely the best things for making good blood and healthy bone and muscle. It was often a trouble to Cricket that he did not grow more rapidly. "If we only lived in the country he would thrive then" was a frequent reflection of hers; but there seemed no probability whatever that little Jack would ever receive the benefit of country air.

One bright September morning Cricket was rather astonished, on coming down stairs, at seeing her father dressed in what he called his "holiday suit."

"Why, father," she said, "are you not going to the docks to-day?"

"Nay, gal," he answered, quite good humouredly,

"I've been working a deal of overtime of late, an' as we're a bit slack just now, I think it's only fair I should have a bit o' a holiday. Don't yer think so ? "

"Well, yes," she answered, slowly. "You have been working very hard lately. I hope you will enjoy yourself very much. Will you be late home ? "

"Ay, most likely I shall. Indeed, ye needn't worrit if I don't turn up for th' night. Very likely I shall go as far as Chester."

Cricket's face fell. She had had plenty of experience of previous holidays, and they had often been the beginning of a drunken "bout" extending over many days. Hence, though she never begrudged her father a holiday, and least of all now, when he had been working so hard, she did tremble for the consequences.

"Ye needn't look so down," he said, noticing the shadow on her face. " I aint a goin' to commit a robbery, or commit suicide."

"On no, I don't suppose you are," she said, with a smile ; " only I do get very anxious when you're out so late."

"Well, ye needn't get anxious to-day, any road," he answered; I'm not going on the fuddle; an' 'ere's a half-crown for yer, if ye an' Jack likes to take a holiday as well."

"Oh, thank you, father!" she answered, a glad smile overspreading her face. "We could have a sail on the river with that, couldn't we?"

"Ay, ye could 'ave a turn at New Brighton," he answered, "an' a donkey-ride inter the bargain."

"Oh, that would be just splendid," she replied. "I've wanted to have a sail on the river ever since we came."

"Well, then, ye can 'ave it to-day," he answered, and, with a hasty "Good morning," he was gone.

Just as Cricket and little Jack were ready to start, Billy Walton put in an appearance.

"Look 'ere, Cricket," he said, "I found a tanner in the middle of the street this morning, so what d'yer say to havin' a turn as far as Birkenhead?"

"Oh, we'll go farther than that, Billy," Cricket answered. "Look at this," and she held out her hand, with the half-crown lying on its palm.

"Turpentine and treacle!" ejaculated Billy.

" Where in the name o' the Catechism did yer get
that ? "

" Father gave it me to have a holiday with," said
Cricket ; " and I'm so glad you've come, for now
we can go together."

" Glory ! " said Billy, " this is better nor goose-
berry tart.   Are ye ready for startin' ? "

" Ay ! if you'd come five minutes later you'd
have found us gone."

"'Deed," said Billy, looking wise, " an' 'ow should
I ha' found yer if yer were gone ? "

Oh, you are sharp this mornin'," said Cricket,
" and there's no time to be wasted in talk of that
sort."

" Well, right you are," answered Billy.   " I allers
gives in to the ladies, so let's be off."

It was a longish walk to the landing stage, and
Jack had to be carried all the way ; but by taking
turns with the little fellow they managed without
difficulty.   Billy and Cricket were both in a high
state of excitement, which was in no degree
lessened when they reached the landing stage, and
found the bell ringing on the New Brighton boat,
previous to the start.

Cricket was in great fear lest they should be left behind ; but Billy was not so easily frightened. "Never fear, Cricket," he whispered to her, "if we look spry we'll be in time yet."

"Come, hurry hup!" shouted the man at the gangway, as, hot and perspiring, the trio drew near. "Hurry hup, or ye'll be left."

"We be 'urrying hup all we can," shouted Billy, making a rush for the boat, with little Jack in his arms. Just in time ; the next minute the gangway went up behind them with a rattle, and the signal was given to the enginemen to start.

It was a bright breezy morning with an incoming tide, and as the long and somewhat narrow vessel cut her way through the waves, and tossed the spray right and left, Cricket could scarcely contain her excitement. To fight the wind and waves in this way was wonderfully exhilarating to her, and brought back again for a brief space the colour to her cheeks.

"Oh, aint it glorious?" she said to her companion, as with parted lips and face aglow, she leaned her elbows on the rail and watched the waves roll swiftly past.

K

"Ay," said Billy, "its splendashus; but look at that big vessel a-lyin' still there, Cricket; I do b'leeve now, that that are Noah's hark."

"Oh no, Billy, it can't be the ark, for the ark weren't built in this country at all," said Cricket.

"Oh, that don't make no difference," said Billy, "it could just float away down 'ere as easy as nothin'"

"Oh no, Billy; that couldn't be," said Cricket, "the ark was built thousands of years ago, an' is all rotted by this."

"Built thousan's o' years ago?" said Billy, in astonishment.

"Ay," said Cricket, "didn't you know that?"

"No," he answered, looking disappointed, "I thought it were a real fresh yarn, but, lor, wot's the use; all them stories as Miss Bute tells us is as stale as last week's pie-crust."

"Well, they are none the worse for that, are they?"

"I should think they are," retorted Billy. "What do I care for folks as was drownded thousan's o' years ago. Here were I ready to pipe my heye las' Sunday, when she were a-tellin' us 'bout Noah

an' the rest on 'em, wi' the houtlandish names, an'
now yer tell me that it all 'appened so long agone
that nobody can tell if there's a word o' truth in
it."

"Oh yes, Billy," said Cricket, looking pained ;
" we know it is all true, 'cause it's in the Bible."

"Well, s'pose it are true," said Billy, " I tell yer
I like a yarn that's a bit fresher, an' I shall tell
Miss Bute so next Sunday," and in this matter
Billy kept his word.

What Billy took to be Noah's ark was a great
"Cunarder" getting ready to sail that afternoon
for New York ; and a monster she looked as she
lay there in midstream, with a number of "coaling-
flats" all around her.

As the ferry-boat sailed close under her bows,
the steerage passengers, who were already on board,
waved their hats and handkerchiefs, and tried to
raise a feeble cheer, but the effort was a failure
Their hearts were too full for mirth or cheering.
They had left home and friends, and were now
about to say good-bye to fatherland. Their faces
were turned towards the sun-set land, where they
were going to make for themselves a new home,

and perhaps a fortune also. But though hope was beating high within their hearts, they had not got over the pain of parting yet. Dear old England was still in sight, and the farewells of their friends still lingered in their ears and in their hearts. They would be glad when the tide was full and they could weigh anchor and steam away across the harbour bar, and turn their faces fairly towards the West. The waiting in the river was only lengthening out the pain of separation.

When Cricket learned that these people, men and women and little children, were emigrants, who had broken up their English homes, and were going away to a strange land beyond the sea, her heart went out to them directly. She understood now why some on board neither waved hand nor handkerchief, why they stood looking over the side of the great vessel with lines of pain upon their faces, and a far-away look in their eyes.

Ah! they were thinking, as she often thought, of the home they had left, and which never more they would see on earth, and wondering what was in store for them when they should land strangers on a foreign shore.

Later in the day, she and Billy watched from the sands of New Brighton the same great vessel steam grandly and swiftly out to sea, watched her till she grew a tiny speck on the horizon, and then they turned and climbed the sand-hills, and when they had reached the highest point they could gain, sat down to view the glorious panorama of land and mountain and sea.

Cricket would have sat there the rest of the day if Billy had let her. She never seemed to tire of the fair face of Nature; every tree and every flower were a joy to her. And now she wanted to store her memory with beautiful pictures, that she might carry them back with her into the murk and gloom of Cooper's Row. It might be many months, or many years, ere she would be able to feast her eyes on such loveliness again, and so wanted to make the most of the opportunity.

But Billy was consumed with a desire to have a donkey-ride on the sands, and as Cricket refused to keep him company in this little entertainment, nothing would satisfy him but that she should come and see what sort of figure he cut.

Cricket readily yielded to his wish in this

matter, and when they reached the "red noses,"
he said :—

" Now, Cricket, you and Jack wait 'ere, an' you'll
see me go ridin' past in about five minits, at the
rate o' a hundred miles a hour."

"All right," Cricket answered, and she sat down
on a boulder, and patiently waited for the performance to begin.

Primed with a sharply pointed bit of wood, which
he carefully hid in his pocket, Billy marched boldly
up to the donkey stand, and, after some considerable haggling as to terms, mounted the largest and
most spirited-looking animal in the group.

" I guess this is your fust ride," said the owner
of the donkey.

"Furst ride be hanged," said Billy, sitting carelessly on the donkey's back ; "do yer take me to
be a greenhorn ? "

Oh no, nothink o' the sort," said the man, with a
sly wink ; "only Ned shies a bit sometimes, but
you'll sit him easy, no doubt."

" Trust me," said Billy ; " I'd sit a helephant."

"Oh, I've no doubt on it," said the man. The
next moment the signal was given, and away went

the donkey, and away went Billy. For the first hundred yards he had to cling to the donkey for dear life; after that, he got a little used to the motion, and began to feel more at ease. A few hundred yards ahead of him he saw Cricket sitting on the boulder, with little Jack on her knee; so he got his bit of wood safely gripped in his right hand, ready for a dash in passing her. The donkey kept up a steady, shambling gait, and, so far, had manifested no disposition to shy. But Billy's desire was to dash past Cricket at a flying gallop. It would never do to go shambling past at the present rate; so he carefully waited his time till nearly opposite where she sat, when he suddenly lifted his right hand, and dug the piece of wood into Neddy's flank.

The attack was so sudden that the donkey started in surprise: the next moment, with nose to the ground, it started off at the speed of the wind, and when just opposite Cricket, stopped suddenly flung its heels high in the air, and sent Billy flying far over its head, into a heap of sand some eight or ten yards in front.

That accomplished, Neddy lifted his head as if

to debate the question, and, seeing his foe lying prostrate, and apparently helpless, in the sand-heap, quickly turned right about face, and galloped back to the stand.

Billy also debated the question, but without lifting his head. He was not much hurt, but he was terribly humiliated. He felt as if he could never face Cricket again, or the owner of the donkey. Had he boasted less at starting, the humiliation would have been less bitter. What should he do? Should he lie there, and pretend to be dead? or should he put a bold face on the matter, and go back to the donkey-owner, and have another try?

Cricket settled the question for him by getting hold of the collar of his jacket, and pulling him out of the sand.

"Are you very much hurt, Billy?" she asked, anxiously.

"Oh no," he answered, "but I'm terrible mad I feel so small. I could eat my ears off for spite. On'y think of it, Cricket."

"Oh, I wouldn't think anything about it if I were you," she said.

"You would if you was in my place," he said.

" An' I thought I were going to cut such a caper too."

" Well, you did cut a caper,," she answered, with a smile.

" Ay," he answered, ruefully, " an' a pretty fool I must ha' looked, flying over a hass's head into a sand-heap. I wonder which looked the biggest hass o' the two."

" Oh, there's no doubt on that score," said Cricket, playfully. " But what do you say to havin' a turn at ham and eggs ? "

" Does yer mean it, Cricket ? "

" Ay, that I do."

" Then I'll say no more 'bout the donkey," he said, flinging up his hat. " An' if I aint up to ridin', by jabbers, you shall see wot I can do at eatin'."

CHAPTER XI.

"SHE LITTLE DREAMED OF WHAT WAS IN STORE FOR HER."

" Oh, teach me in the trying hour,
    When anguish swells the dewy tear,
To still my sorrows, own Thy power,
    Thy goodness love, Thy justice fear."

CHATTERTON.

NEITHER Cricket nor Billy soon forgot that day at New Brighton. It was like a bright, brief summer in the perpetual winter of their lives, and in the dreary weeks and months that followed the memory of it was a constant source of pleasure to them.

Poor Cricket little dreamed what was in store for her when she laughed and chatted with Billy over their late dinner of ham and eggs. Had she known there would have been no mirth nor sunshine

But not even a shadow of a suspicion crossed her mind, and when, on the following day, her father returned accompanied by a low, vulgar-looking woman, and announced to Cricket that this was her new mother, she sank back in her chair completely overcome, and for a while neither spoke nor moved.

"Come, come, yer needn't glower like that," said her father, somewhat angrily, at length. "Get up an' kiss yer new mother, an' tell her she's welcome."

Mechanically Cricket tried to obey, but the new Mrs. Chase checked her advance.

"No, young miss," she said, indignantly; "I'll have none o' yer kisses; but I'll bring ye to yer senses in a week, never fear."

And in this she kept her vow. From that day forward Cricket's life was a perpetual martyrdom. Nothing that she could do would please the newcomer. If she smiled a welcome, the smile was interpreted as one of scorn or contempt. If she spoke pleasantly, her words and tone were purposely misconstrued. If she offered her assistance in any matter, it was always rejected, until at length she gave up trying to please, and prayed that she might die.

From the very first moment of their meeting they took a dislike to each other—a dislike which the flight of time only strengthened and intensified. Cricket tried her best to hide her instinctive abhorrence of the woman who had come to usurp her mother's place, but she could not always succeed. Mrs. Chase was not slow to gauge the state of the girl's heart, and resolved to have her revenge.

" The impudent minx," she said to herself, " she thinks she's agoin' to rule me, but I'll soon make her knuckle under ; an' if I don't bend her proud neck, I'll break it, that's all." And she was not a woman that was in the habit of being thwarted. She had made up her mind soon after she met Richard Chase that he should ask her to be his wife, and she dogged his steps until she had gained her end. He was as clay in her hands ; he knew he would be before he married her ; but somehow (he did not know how, and he could never find out) he was in a trap, and, as far as he could see, there was no way of escape. So, in his heavy, stolid way, he quietly submitted to the inevitable, and tried to persuade himself that it was the best thing after all.

Little Jack took to her amazingly, and she to him ; there was something in the little fellow's bonny face and happy childish ways that touched even her coarse nature, and called into play its better side. She carried him about with her as a school girl might a new doll, and when she discovered what a joy he was to Cricket, out of sheer spite, she took charge of him by night as well as day, and left poor Cricket, with breaking heart, to spend her nights alone.

Cricket bore this in silence ; she felt that it was useless making complaints. But one day, when she saw her stepmother teaching little Jack to drink whiskey-toddy out of her glass, she could keep silent no longer. Of all things in the world, she dreaded strong drink the most. If she had seen her stepmother giving Jack laudanum she could not have been more horrified, So, without thinking of consequences, she marched up close to her stepmother's elbow, and said, pleadingly, " Oh, please don't ; give him anything but—"

But the sentence was never finished ; a back-handed slap across her face, that loosened two of her front teeth, silenced her in a moment, while, by way of further revenge, Jack was treated to a second and a larger helping of whiskey-toddy.

At first the little fellow pulled awful faces at the taste of spirits of every kind. But his prejudices were soon overcome, and by Christmas he would search among the glasses that were within his reach, in the hope of finding a few drops at the bottom.

This, coupled with the treatment she constantly received at the hands of the brutal woman she was compelled to call " mother," nearly broke Cricket's heart. All the roses faded from her cheek and the sunshine from her smile, and the only thing she prayed for was, that God might take her and little Jack to the better country, where they might find their own mother again, and dwell for ever beyond the reach of sin and sorrow.

Now and then Richard Chase remonstrated with his wife, and endeavoured to protect Cricket from her cruelty. But his interference only made matters worse ; when he was out of the way Cricket was accused of telling tales to her father, and was punished with two-fold severity. Slaps and abuse she could have borne, but when she was kept sometimes for a whole day without food, and even the clothing taken from her bed at night, her health as well as her spirits began to fail her. The only respite she could be certain of was on a Saturday evening, when she knew that both her father and stepmother would be at some public-house in the neighbourhood, and frequently little Jack kept them company.

That was the only night also that Billy ventured to put in an appearance at No. 13. And as he frequently got what he termed "a hodd job," in running errands on a Saturday evening, it was not very much that he saw of his friend. He was always welcome, however, whenever he did come. His presence was as medicine to Cricket : while listening to the story of Billy's adventures, and his hard struggles with the world she would often forget her own pain and heartache, and feel for a little while her old interest in life come back to her.

She saw very little of him on a Sunday now, for she could go to church and Sunday-school only by stealth ; moreover, her clothes were so worn and shabby that she was almost ashamed to go.

She did not even tell Billy all she had to bear from day to day : the petty annoyances, the jealousies, and abuse. But he knew without being told that she was having what he termed " a 'ard time o' it," and he did all he could to cheer her whenever he had an opportunity.

So time went on, and matters got worse and worse at No. 13. There was no longer any semblance or even pretence of affection between husband and wife. Comfort in the home there was none, and the only pleasure sought for was in the wine-bottle. Sometimes the neighbours " clubbed together" and spent a whole night in a drunken carousal, while Cricket waited alone in the desolate house, not having the company even of little Jack.

What she suffered during these weary days and nights no words can tell. Life to her was one long martyrdom, a perpetual pain, unrelieved by a single ray of hope of better days in store.

After Christmas trade got bad again, which meant to Richard Chase, and to many another man, more time to spend in the public-house, and more misery at home.

However small the weekly wage might be the publican always got his share. It was no wonder the drink traffic held its own, in spite of depressed trade, when drink was the last luxury to be given up, and men and women starved their children and even pawned their clothes to gratify an accursed thirst for gin.

Poor Cricket was the first to feel the pinch of bad times. Mrs. Chase was heard to declare again and again that " she cared mighty little about vittels, as long as she could 'ave her drop to sup." And while her husband earned anything at all she got her " sup," and he got his also.

But food was often scarce at No. 13 ; and often Cricket went supperless to bed and cried herself to sleep, and awoke next morning to find that there was not a crust in the house for breakfast.

Jack generally fared better. If there was any food in the house at all, Mrs. Chase was always careful that he should eat his fill ere Cricket touched a morsel. Cricket never complained at that ; indeed she would rather suffer hunger a hundred times herself, than that little Jack should cry for bread. But what cut her to the heart was to see how eagerly he drank the poisonous liquor that was given to him every day. " He will grow up a drunkard," she said, and indeed it was difficult to see how it could be otherwise.

Sometimes she was tempted, when they were alone together, to take the child in her arms, and run away with him out into the wide world—to tramp her way across the mountains to Cefn Lee and ask her grand-parents' help and protection, and had it been any other time than winter she might have yielded to the impulse.

It was not often, however, that she was alone with Jack. Mrs. Chase generally took him with her when she went visiting among her neighbours, and these visits generally extended far into the night, and sometimes indeed till the following morning.

So the winter slowly wore itself away. Early in February Levi was seized with an attack of bronchitis, which kept him in the house nearly three months, depriving Billy not only of his company and counsel, but also of the shelter afforded by the furnace room, and the weekly wage received for helping to dust the church.

Billy began to feel the pinch of bad times in a way he had not known now for more than a year. Often at the close of the day he found himself with a solitary copper, and it became a question whether he should spend it in purchasing supper or in paying for a night's lodging. Either alternative was a painful one, for the nights were cold and stormy, and sheltered corners were not easy to find. And yet to huddle hungry on a bundle of dirty straw, with several other lads, was scarcely more inviting. And then, to make matters worse, his clothes had become so ragged that he did not dare, under any circumstances, to take them off, knowing full well that if he did, he would never find his way into them again. On the whole, therefore, the year was beginning badly for him, while his faith in the good policy of honesty was becoming sadly shaken, and but for the influence of Cricket he would have gone back to the old ways again.

Nearly the only comfort he had now was in reading old newspapers that fell in his way. He had mastered the art of reading with astounding rapidity, and he held it fast by continual practice,

while his affection for a few old books that Levi
had given him was remarkable ; no hunger nor
want could tempt him to sell them.

So—as I have stated before—the winter wore
slowly away, and March came in blustering and
cold. There was no improvement in trade, nor in
the habits of Richard and Jenifer Chase. Nearly
all the money the former earned was spent in
drink, and, as a consequence, food became scarcer
all the while.

One bitterly cold evening about the middle of
March Cricket was sent on an errand to Bootle,
and when she returned, hungry and tired, she
found the house in darkness, and the door locked.
That her stepmother would purposely lock her
out she could scarcely believe. Perhaps she was
not expected back so soon, and in the meanwhile
her stepmother had gone into the house of one of
the neighbours.

So Cricket went from door to door making
inquiries, but everywhere received the same
answer—Mrs. Chase had not been seen for the
evening.

Getting tired at length of tramping up and down

the streets and receiving no invitation from any of
the neighbours to come in and rest—for she did
not explain that her own door was locked against
her—she sat herself down on the door-step of No.
13, in the teeth of a bitter east wind, to wait the
return of her parents.

She was feeling very desolate, for not only was
she cold and hungry, but she was almost heart-
broken as well. Slowly the tears gathered in her
eyes, as she thought of the old days back in the
quiet country. She tried to brush them away, but
they came all the faster, and at length began to
drop like slow rain upon her lap.

She did not heed the patter of bare feet along
the court, nor was she aware of Billy's presence till
he stood before her.

" Cricket," he said, in a low tone, " wot are ye
doin' 'ere in the cold ? "

She was unable to speak for a little time, then,
choking back her sobs, she answered, " The door's
locked against me."

He gave a low whistle, but made no other
answer for a little while. Then, sitting down
beside her, he said, " I'm in the same box,

Cricket, so I'll stay with yer, an' 'elp an' keep yer warm."

For a while they sat in silence, but when Billy spoke again, his teeth were chattering so, that Cricket could scarcely make out what he said.

"Billy," she said, "you'll be froze in those rags. Come into the corner, and let me sit on the outside."

"Oh no," he said, with a poor attempt at a laugh, "it ain't nothin', Cricket; an' I'se used to it."

"Then you shall have my shawl," she said; "my clothes are much warmer than yours."

"No, no, Cricket!" he said, putting up his hand, "I don't mind a bit."

"But you *shall* have my shawl," she answered, "you'll starve an' die. Now not another word. There, that's better; now come up close to me."

He made no further attempt at resistance; indeed, he was only too glad to obey. So there in the bitter, boisterous night they sat side by side, waiting and longing for the morning.

CHAPTER XII.

"'I HAVE ONLY ONE CARE,' SHE SAID."

" Oh ! many are the mansions there,
But not in one hath grief a share !
No haunting shade from things gone by
May there o'ersweep th' unchanging sky."

HEMANS.

WATCHING for the morning proved to be what Billy called "a slow bizness," and not long after midnight he fell into a sound sleep, with his head resting against Cricket's shoulder. For a long time, with her eyes fixed upon the shining stars, that burned in the long strip of sky above the narrow street, she listened to Billy's regular breathing. Her senses were too numbed to think much or even fret, and so, unconsciously, she dropped off at length into a troubled sleep, in which fearful dreams haunted her, and robbed repose of all its healing power.

The first glimmer of the morning was appearing above the housetops, when she awoke with a start, feeling as though her head were on fire, while her teeth were chattering with cold.

" Oh dear," she moaned, raising her hands and pressing them to her temples, " what can be the matter with me ? I never felt like this before in my life."

"Wot's hup," said Billy, at length opening his eyes with a yawn ; aint ye very well, Cricket ?"

" Oh, I don't know, Billy," she said. " I'm burnin' hot an' chattering cold at the same time."

" Oh, yer only wants a run," said Billy, hopefully. " Let's get up from 'ere an' 'ave a run inter Bunter Street, and ye'll be all right in no time."

" Do you think so ? " she said, wearily. " I feel as if I didn't want to move."

" Oh, I've feel'd that way millions o' times," said Billy. " Ye ain't used to sleepin' in the hopen hair, but it's nothin' when ye gets inter the way o' it."

" Oh dear," said Cricket, struggling to her feet. " I don't think I can run, Billy ; I'm stiff all over, and everything is all of a swim."

" Oh, don't you mind that," said Billy, giving her his hand. " Now, one, two, three, and a hoff."

For Cricket, however, running was out of the question. She did her best, but she reeled from side to side, as though she were drunk, and but that Billy held her hand tightly, she would have fallen.

" I fear, Cricket," he said at length, in tones of real distress, " that ye are wuss than I took yer to be."

" Oh, I don't know," she answered, staggering on in a dazed, helpless kind of way ; " perhaps I'll feel better after a bit."

" It's all my fault," moaned Billy, " every bit on it. I never ought to ha' took that shawl. It were real mean of me."

" Oh, no, Billy ; don't say that," she replied ; " your clothes are so ragged as to be as bad as none at all."

" But I'se used to it," he replied, " an' ye aint. But I didn't think, Cricket, ye were agoin' to get ill, or I'd never ha' took it. I really wouldn't, Cricket."

"You'll make me worse, Billy," she answered, "if you blame yourself that way. I couldn't have kept the shawl when your chest and shoulders were bare to the wind."

"Oh, ye're too good, Cricket," Billy answered; "I aint worth haaf the trouble."

She made no answer to that, but caught away her hand suddenly from Billy's grasp, and raised both hands to her throbbing head; the next moment she reeled and fell, striking her forehead heavily on the stone flags.

Billy rushed to her assistance in a moment, and tried to raise her up; but she was a dead weight on his hands, and he found it impossible to render her any assistance. Up and down the street he looked eagerly, but not a soul was in sight,

"Cricket," he called, but she gave no answer. Her face was white and drawn; her eyes closed; her lips covered with foam.

"Oh, Cricket," he moaned, "be you very ill, Cricket, or be you dead? oh, do just speak an' tell me!"

But there came no answer to his anxious inquiry. Then Billy raised his voice to its highest pitch, and called, "Help, help, help!" and soon after the burly form of a policeman loomed into sight.

A few words of explanation from Billy, and the policeman sprang his rattle, and was soon joined by a brother officer. A few minutes later, a stretcher was secured, and poor Cricket, still unconscious, was carried to the Northern Hospital.

Billy followed like one in a dream. He saw the great door of the hospital open, and heard it close behind him, as he followed close upon the policeman's heels. Up the broad flight of stairs he went, as though he trod on air, for he heard no sound, and saw nothing save the policeman's heavy form before him; then another door opened, and, ere he could enter, was shut in his face.

How long he remained outside he never knew He saw the policeman come out and walk away. He saw several other people come and go, but no one seemed to take any notice of him, or ask him what he wanted, or why he was there.

At length a gentleman stood before him. Billy learnt afterwards that it was one of the doctors.

"You are the girl's brother?" he said. To which Billy shook his head by way of reply.

"But you know her?" the doctor asked.

"Oh, aye!" said Billy, eagerly, "I should think I does. Is she 'most ready to go home."

The doctor smiled as he answered, "She is very ill, very ill, indeed. Now, I want you to tell me all you know about her, and where she lives, and all that."

Then followed a string of questions, all of which he answered to the best of his ability.

Half-an-hour later Billy found himself standing in the street gazing helplessly at the great dingy building before him. What did it all mean? was the question he debated with himself. Was he awake or dreaming? What was all that he had heard about "high fever," "inflammation of the lungs," "badly nourished state," and a lot of other things he could neither make head nor tail of.

Could it be really true that Cricket was lying ill in that great house, perhaps dying, and that he could not see her again till the next day but one.

He was some time ere he could realize all the truth, and when he did so, he turned away with a great sob, though where he should go or what he should do he had not the remotest idea. How he

spent that day and the next, with the two weary
nights that followed, he never knew. Nor did he
know till then how much Cricket was to him, nor
how deeply her goodness and gentleness had
touched his heart. In his greatest misery and need
she had been more than a sister to him, her bonny
face made for him perpetual sunshine, and the
tones of her voice were always as music in his ears
and in his heart also. She listened to the story of
his troubles, and tried to comfort him when her
own heart was breaking; and had given him food
to eat while she went hungry herself, and yet he
was nothing to her, neither kith nor kin. This
kindness to a stranger was always a mystery to
him, and the more he thought of it the more his
wonder and reverence grew. He felt sometimes as
if he could go and kneel down at her feet and
worship her, and was amazed and indignant that
her father should treat her with so much indifference and neglect.

Once he started up from his reverie and rushed
off to Cooper's Row.

"It must be all a dream," he said to himself;
"any road I'll go an' 'ave a peep."

From the opposite side of the court he watched the house for a quarter of an hour. He saw little Jack playing about the door-step, heard him try to pronounce the name of Cricket more than once, and saw him look round, as if expecting she would come. Saw his stepmother come up the court with a large jug of beer in her hands, and heard her call from within, " Come, Jackey, for a sup." Saw the little fellow creep hurriedly up the steps on his hands and knees, and disappear within the house in answer to her call, and then, sick at heart, Billy turned away, muttering to himself, " It's all true, Cricket aint there."

Nevertheless he was not without hope that she would soon be back again in the old place, and hence was quite unprepared for the news that awaited him at the hospital.

" Will she soon be better ? " was his first question to the nurse who was to conduct him to Cricket's bedside, and there was so much of eager, painful anxiety in the tones of his voice, that she looked at him again before replying. What a forlorn little creature he looked. A mere bundle of rags ; tear-stained, dust-stained, with a world of pleading in his hunger-hollowed eyes, and a tremour about the lips, that went direct to the woman's heart.

"You are not her brother?" she said.

"No," he answered, "I'm nothin' to 'er, but she's everythink to me."

"Then I'm very sorry for you," the nurse answered, "for I fear she cannot get better."

"Does yer mean by that, that she will die?" he asked.

"I fear so," she replied.

And without another word she conducted him to Cricket's bedside. She did not see him; with closed eyes she lay, panting like a stricken hare. Her face was flushed, her lips apart, her breath came and went in quick short gasps.

Billy sat down by her bedstead without a word. He could not trust himself to speak to her as yet, but he reached out his hand at length, and took her hot hand in his. She opened her eyes at that, and when she saw Billy a smile broke out all over her face like a burst of summer's sunshine.

"Oh, Billy," she said, "I'm so glad you've come."

He did not reply, but the hot tears welled up in

his eyes in a moment and rolled silently down his cheeks.

" Don't cry, Billy," she said, catching sight of his tears and quivering lips. " I'm glad we've known each other. We'll be together again in heaven."

" I dunno 'bout that," he sobbed ; " I fear heaven ain't mich in my road."

" Oh, yes," she said, " heaven is for everybody that trusts in the Saviour an' tries to be good."

" I reckon its easy for you to be good," he said, " I don't think ye could be bad if ye were to try, Cricket. But I'm made o' hawful dirt."

" Don't say that, Billy," she answered slowly, for it was difficult for her to speak at all. " The good Lord has died for us all, the bad and good alike."

He made no reply to that, and after awhile she went on again.

" I'm glad to go, Billy, for mother's up in heaven looking out for me, an' I know she'll be glad to have me with her ; an' since *she* came—you know who I mean, Billy—home ain't been home no longer."

" Aye, I knows," he said, with a great sob.

" But there'll be no trouble, nor hunger, nor cold

in heaven," she said, closing her eyes ; " and, oh, I know I shall be happy there."

For awhile no other word was spoken. Steadily the silent tears kept rolling down Billy's cheeks and dropped like slow rain upon the floor.

" I have only one care," she said at length, opening her eyes again, " and that is little Jack. I should have run away with him an' tried to find Grandfather Evans at Cefn-Lee, had it been summer instead of winter, but the good Lord knows best."

" I seen little Jack, yesterday," said Billy brokenly.

" My little darling," she answered ; and now the tears came into her eyes.

" Oh, Billy," she said, " if you will promise to be a friend to little Jack, I shall die in peace."

" Cricket," he answered, slowly and with a great effort, " Jack shall never want a frien' while I can 'elp 'im."

She grasped his hand in silence at that, but made no further reply.

It was time for Billy to go, but still he hesitated. He felt somehow that this was their last meeting.

M

He had said good-bye, and still he waited, holding her hand tightly in his. She noticed his hesitancy and asked him, at length, if he had anything more to say.

He did not speak for a moment, then gulping down a great lump in his throat, he said :—

" You've been **very** good to me, Cricket, better nor anybody else in the world, an' ye're going away now, cause yer would keep me warm wi' yer own shawl. I never 'ad no sister, Cricket, an' nobody to love me afore ye found me, an' now I should like to kiss yer afore ye died. It 'ud comfort me when ye're gone, Cricket."

She smiled in answer, such a smile as Billy never forgot, and bending his head he pressed his lips tightly on her forehead. She felt his scalding tears falling like rain upon her face, and then without another word he glided silently and swiftly away.

CHAPTER XIII.

"I WANT TO BE WITH CRICKET."

> " Hide me, O twilight air !
> Hide me from thought, from care,
> From all things foul or fair,
>   Until to-morrow !
> To-night I strive no more;
> No more my soul shall soar :
> Come, sleep, and shut the door
>   'Gainst pain and sorrow ! "
>
> PROCTOR.

N the following afternoon Billy was again at the hospital. He knew it was not visitors' day, but he was impatient to know the fate of Cricket, and, at the risk of being driven away from the door, he gave the bell a vigorous pull, and waited.

The door was quickly opened, and nearly shut again in his face, ere he could offer any explanation of his visit.

" This is not visitors' day," said the young man, on seeing that there was no patient requiring admission.

" Aye, I know that," said Billy, eagerly; " but I'm dying to know how Cricket are. Could yer jist tell me now if she's better ? "

" Is Cricket your sister ? " the young man asked, somewhat impatiently.

" Oh, no : but she's nearly the on'y frien' I've in the world," said Billy, wistfully; " an' she were powerful ill yesterday."

" Oh, you mean the little girl that was brought in so badly hurt," said the attendant, in more sympathetic tones.

" Aye, that's her," said Billy, eagerly ; " she got a terrible bumper agin the flags. Is she gettin' better, do you know ? "

The attendant shook his head, and Billy felt his heart stand still ; and for several moments they stood looking at each other, as though neither liked to break the silence.

Billy was the first to speak. " Then she's worse ? " he gasped.

" I'm very sorry for you," said the attendant

kindly, "but she died this morning about nine o'clock."

Billy grasped the door handle suddenly, as a momentary numbness crept over him. But it was only for a moment. By a strong effort of will, he shook off the feeling, and drew himself up to his full height ; but he was pale to the very lips.

"Yer say she's dead !" he said, in a voice that he could not recognise as his own, looking the attendant straight in the face at the same time.

"Yes, my lad. I'm very sorry for you."

And without another word being spoken, the door was pulled open, and Billy passed silently out into the street. It was a bright, breezy March afternoon, with a clear sky and a warm south wind. Everywhere people were congratulating each other and themselves on the sudden change in the weather, and hopes were entertained on every hand that after the long "spell of east wind," the warm weather would last—a hope, however, which was soon dispelled.

Poor Billy, however, neither saw the sunshine nor felt its genial warmth. The world to him had become suddenly dark, and never did life seem to him so cheerless or so full of pain as it did that day. All unconsciously, and almost blindly, he hurried on through the crowded streets, seeing nothing and hearing nothing, and with no definite object before him. All that he most feared and dreaded had happened. Cricket was dead and Levi was ill, and he was left without a friend in all the world. He did not weep : his grief just then was too great for tears. But he felt stunned, bewildered, crushed. Why he kept hurrying on through the streets he did not know, except that he had a vague feeling that he must do something. He could not reason about anything. He was walking as though in a dream, and will he had none.

When he did stop, it was with a sudden shock as though he had been awakened suddenly. He had reached the river wall, and before him the deep, full river swept outward towards the sea, bearing upon its strong bosom such a crowd of shipping as perhaps no other river can show. Atlantic liners, Australian clippers, huge wooden coasters, pilot boats, ferry boats, tug boats, barges and flats, all crowded pell-mell upon its heaving waters, passing and re-passing each other, up the river, down the river, across the river, making a scene at once of repose and of animation. The sight had a wonderfully soothing effect upon Billy. He had seen the picture many times before, but he never got tired of it. Every day the great river seemed to have something new and fresh.

With his feet overhanging the swiftly rushing water he sat down to watch the great liners steam gracefully outwards bearing their precious freights of human lives, to lands beyond the great sea that stretched away in the distance.

Past the New Brighton pier he watched them glide on, and away, growing smaller and smaller till they seemed but a speck on the far-off horizon, and then they vanished altogether from view.

Billy heaved a great sigh when the last spar had disappeared, then said, half aloud :—

"Cricket's gone like that ; gone away to a country that's out o' sight. The ships'll come 'ome again, but Cricket never will, never no more. Oh, Cricket ! an' to think yer should have died for me !" and Billy burst into a flood of tears, the first he had shed for the day.

Billy could not get over the conviction that Cricket had given her life for him. "If she had kep' the shawl herself instead o' wrapping me in it, she'd ha' been living still," he moaned. "Oh, Cricket! Cricket!"

That generous act of Cricket's was a revelation to him in more senses than one. He had never believed the gospel story till now. How often he had smiled at Cricket in a superior kind of way when she had told him the story of the Cross, and had shaken his head in token that he did not believe it. But to-day it all came back to him with a new meaning and with a wealth of evidence he could not resist. If Cricket had given her life for him, it was no longer a thing incredible that Christ should die for all the race. This much was clear to him. It was a "beam in darkness" and was sure to grow.

It was late in the afternoon when he left the river wall, and made his way towards Cooper's Row. He had no definite plan in his mind. He had long come to the conclusion that it was not of much use planning anything. He had to take things as they came and make the best of them.

He never knew what might turn up; but he was generally on the look-out in case anything should turn up to his advantage. At present, however, he was thinking less of himself than of Cricket's little brother Jack, and wondering if ever it would be in his power to befriend the little fellow, who was Cricket's last thought and care.

The promise he had made only the previous afternoon was not one lightly to be passed over or soon forgotten. Perhaps he had been foolish in making any promise at all of any kind. For, after all what could he do to befriend Jack, even if the little fellow should be in need? To take care of himself was more than he could well manage, and hence the idea of helping anybody else seemed absurd.

Still, the promise had been made, and if only for Cricket's sake, and out of love and respect for her memory, he would keep his eye on her little brother. No harm could come of that, and it might be that good would come.

So he made his way with slow and weary steps towards Cooper's Row. He was very hungry, very weary, and very sad. He heeded nothing that

was passing around him, he sought no employ
ment, he asked no alms.   But his sad and suffering
face touched more than one heart that afternoon
and more than one copper was pressed upon him.
Indeed, in one case a shilling was given to him,
and ere he could recover his astonishment or ex-
press his thanks his benefactor was gone.

Something was turning up, truly.   Could it be
that God cared for him, as Cricket had so often
told him He did?   Was there anything in Providence after all?   He was greatly puzzled and yet
greatly comforted at these unexpected touches of
kindness.   He did not know that the mute appeal
of his suffering face was more eloquent than any
words could be.   And so it came about that he
found himself in possession of sixteen pence, but
was altogether at a loss how to account for the
fact.

He found little Jack Chase sitting on the door-
step " waiting for Cricket," as the child expressed
it.   He came to Billy in a moment with a glad
smile upon his face.   " I want Cricket," were his
first words.   " Won't she be coming back soon,
Billy ? "

"I fear not," said Billy, gulping down a great lump that had risen in his throat. "She were powerful ill when I seen 'er last."

"Then take me to her," the child pleaded. "I do want Cricket"

"Does yer want to go away from 'ere," said Billy, eagerly, as though a new idea had struck him.

"Aye," he answered, "I want to be with Cricket."

Billy did not answer for a moment, then, speaking more to himself than to the child, he said, "Ye'd be a mighty sight better off if ye were with 'er, I'm thinkin'. But ye'll have to wait yer turn," and Billy brushed his hand quickly across his eyes to hide the gathering tears.

"I wish I could go to-night," said the child.

"I wish yer could," was the answer, "an' me too, for as Levi used to say ' there's nowt but trouble an' comfort 'ere,' though wot the comfort are, I know no more than a helephant."

For nearly an hour Billy sat on the doorstep with little Jack upon his knee. Then Mrs. Chase was seen reeling up the court in a state of intoxication.

Billy was ordered to leave the court "immejet," if he did not wish to have every bone in his skin broken, while Jack was saluted with a box on the ear for associating with "sich ragged varmints" as Billy.

Jack set up a great yell and tried to run after Billy, but in this was prevented by his stepmother, who dragged him screaming up the steps into the house.

Billy's reflection, as he wended his way along Bunter Street, in search of a place where he could get supper and spend the night was, "The little chap must be got away from that woman. She aint 'is mother, an' is spoilin' 'im hout an' hout. I dunno 'ow it are to be done, but if summot don't turn hup I'll turn up sommot myself. It were Cricket's wish, an' I'll do it, or my name aint Billy Walton."

Having come to this conclusion he quickened his steps, and after nearly half an hour's walk found the place he was in search of. It was not a very inviting spot. Places that provide supper, bed and breakfast for sixpence are not usually very inviting. After supper Billy spent an extra twopence in a stamp, sheet of paper, and an envelope, and, borrowing pen and ink from the mistress of the establishment, made his first attempt at letter writing.

He could read very well, and rarely stumbled at the longest words, but writing was a very different matter, and "spelling," as he discovered, was not such an easy matter as he had imagined.

As is often the case with amateurs, Billy commenced by addressing the envelope, and printed each letter in his best style. This is what the envelope bore when Billy had finished :—

Maister an Missus Chace

13 *Coopers Row*

Hoff Bunters Strete

Liverpool

CHAPTER XIV.

"IT BEATS ALL CREATION."

" I do not think where'er thou art,
    Thou hast forgotten me ;
And I perhaps, may soothe this heart
    In thinking too of thee :
Yet there was round thee such a dawn
    Of light ne'er seen before,
As fancy never could have drawn,
    And never can restore."
WOLFE.

HE letter took Billy a full hour to complete, and ran as follows :—

"You don't need to trubbel 'bout littel Jack. I'le take kare hoff 'im. Cricket ast me to do it. She said hee hud be a drunker if he stay. Nobbody shall 'arm 'im. So you don't need to be tole hankshus 'bout 'im. Jack likes me, Hi likes 'im.

" BILLY WALTON."

Billy read and re-read this letter after he had

finished it, scanned the formation of each word with critical eye, and then with a grunt of satis-faction, folded it up carefully and placed it in the envelope. Carefully wrapping this again, in a half sheet of newspaper, he put the whole package in his pocket and prepared for bed.

The letter was not to be posted yet. He must get possession of Jack first ; and before he made any attempt in that direction he must earn some more money. So, early next morning he started off to Lime Street Station. He had an impression that if it were right for him to take charge of little Jack, and convey him all the way to Cefn Lee, the means would be forthcoming somehow.

Since yesterday his faith in Providence had grown in a remarkable degree. His experience on the previous day had been such a strange one. Money had come to him so freely. Little Jack had been so delighted at seeing him, and had caught at the idea of going away from Cooper's Row with so much pleasure, that his scepticism in regard to Providence had broken down completely, and he was quite ready to adopt Cricket's view of the matter in its entirety.

Now, during that forenoon a curious scene was enacted in St. George's Hall, and was recorded in the " Local Intelligence " column of all the Liverpool newspapers. The paragraph was headed " A strange Scene in St. George's Hall," and went on to say how an elderly gentleman whose name had not transpired, had gathered round him some twenty or thirty of the most ragged and neglected children to be found in the neighbourhood of Lime Street, had taken them into St. George's Hall, stripped them of their dirty rags, and had attired each lad in a bran new suit of clothes of some strong and warm material.

That Billy—being in Lime Street, at the time— should be included in the number, is not to be wondered at, for in the matter of rags he carried off the palm, and so was the first object of the gentleman's charity. Perhaps it was the sight of Billy, that suggested the scene recorded. Of that we do not know. Certain it is, however, that Billy, along with twenty-five other lads, found himself for the first time in his life attired in a bran new suit of warm and easy-fitting clothes; and all of a sudden became conscious of a dignity that up to that time he did not know he possessed.

Perhaps it was the particularly woe-begone appearance of our hero that led to the further gift in Billy's case of a half-crown. So bewildered was Billy by the whole ceremony, that he never knew if he thanked the gentleman for his bounty or not. Indeed, he was not quite certain for some time if he was awake, and when he saw his reflection a few minutes later in a shop window, he rubbed his eyes again and again, and changed his position a dozen times over, and then walked across the street, and took a peep at himself in another shop window, before he could be convinced that it was his own self he saw reflected.

The last seen of the gentleman who had proved himself such a friend, he was standing on the steps of the great hall, and leaning against one of the pillars, watching, with a pleased smile on his benevolent face, the lads, as they rushed hither and thither, proud to show off their new clothes, and carrying their chins six inches higher than they had ever done before in their lives. To the best of our knowledge, he has never yet revealed his name. But that he has had his reward there can be no doubt, and the memory of that day must be to him an abiding spring of pleasure and satisfaction.

Much has been said and written on the "Philosophy of Clothes." Billy's experience, if fully written out, would prove an interesting contribution to the subject. It seemed to him that as great a change had been wrought inwardly as outwardly. He felt as though he stood on a higher moral plane. The idea of doing anything mean never seemed to him so repugnant before.

"Blow me," he said to himself, regarding his reflection in a shop window with much complacency and with evident satisfaction, "if I'm not a gent at last; I never did think I could be made into sich a swell. Bless my soul an' stockings, if I don't feel as good as the Prince o' Wales. And in course I'll 'ave to hact like a gent now. It ud never do to disgrace cloas o' this cut. Wouldn't Cricket be delighted now if she was to get a squint at me," and the tears welled up into his eyes in a moment, and ere he could wipe them away had fallen upon his cheek.

He did not seek to earn any more money that day ; with three shillings in his possession, and the letter in his pocket, which he had been careful to transfer from the old clothes to the new, he made his way with all possible haste to Cooper's Row.

That it was his duty to take charge of little Jack he had now no longer the least shadow of a doubt. Everything seemed to point in one direction.

" To think I should ha' been in Lime Street just at the very nick o' time," he said to himself. " It beats all Creation, an' to think the gent should ha' gived me the money besides the cloas. Its like the Harabian Nights, an' Sinbad the Sailor, and Jack the Giant Killer, all rolled into one. I'll never laugh at nothin' no more in the Bible arter this."

Billy's last lingering doubt respecting Providence had been removed by the events of this morning. And with his new found faith and hope he was able to contemplate the future with a degree of peace and satisfaction he had never known before.

" Poor Cricket," he said softly to himself, his eyes growing moist the while. " I ken understan' now why she were always so 'appy an' why she took her

trubbels so content, she knowed the good God ud
take care o' her ; an' He did take care o 'er, an' now
she's in the better country as she were always a
talkin' about, an' is 'appy for hever wi' nobody to
abuse her or make her cry.   Oh, Cricket! Cricket!"
and Billy sat down on a door step and hid his face
in his hands, and for five minutes cried softly to
himself.   Then springing to his feet and brushing
his hand quickly across his eyes, he started off with
a run, as though determined to make up for lost
time.

It was scarcely past noon, when he reached
Cooper's Row.   Little Jack, as on the day before,
was sitting on the steps "waiting for Cricket."
He did not recognise Billy at first, so great was
the change the new clothes had produced.
But when Billy spoke his face brightened in a
moment.

" Oh, Billy," he said, "you'll take me to Cricket
to-day, won't you ? "

" Not to-day, Jackey," Billy answered,   " But I'll
take yer somewhere else if you'll go."

"Oh yes, I'll go," the child answered instantly,
and slipped off the steps in a trice.

"Is yer mother about?" asked Billy in a whisper.

"No, she's gone up to the 'George'" the child answered with quaint glibness.

"Will she be long away!" Billy asked next.

"Oh, no, only five minutes," was the answer.

For a moment Billy stood biting his lip not knowing what course to pursue. The court was alive with boys and girls and little children, even babies were sprawling in the gutters. To get Jack away therefore without being observed, and to get him away before Mrs. Chase returned, was the task before him. How was it to be done?

His hesitation only lasted a moment. "Come inter the 'ouse, Jackey," he said in a whisper. Behind the door a small shawl was hanging, a kind of heir-loom in the family. He had seen Cricket in the old days put it over the child's shoulders, cross it over his chest and tie the ends or corners at the back. Billy followed her example in this matter and succeeded without the least difficulty.

"Now, Jackey, where's your cap?" he asked excitedly, for he dreaded every moment the return of Mrs. Chase.

"Up there," said the child, pointing with his forefinger to a cap hanging on a hook close up to the ceiling.

By the aid of a broom-handle the cap was soon secured and placed on Jack's head.

"Now Jackey, we're ready," said Billy in a whisper. "Now listen to me an' do what I tell yer——" before he could proceed further with his speech, however, he was startled by the sound of heavy footsteps on the flags outside.

"Here's mother," said Jack as a heavy form filled the doorway, while Billy slunk under the table in terror.

CHAPTER XV.

"WILL SHE FIND US IN THE DARK?"

" Dear beauteous death ! the jewel of the just,
   Shining nowhere but in the dark ;
What mysteries do lie beyond thy dust,
   Could man outlook that mark ! "

VAUGHAN.

ACK'S words, however, proved a false alarm. The figure in the door-way was not that of Mrs. Chase, but of a neighbour, who had come across for an hour's gossip. Finding, however, that Mrs. Chase was not at home, she turned away at once, remarking that she would run across during the afternoon.

As soon as she was gone, Billy crept out from under the table looking as pale as a ghost.

" By jabbers," he said, " I've 'ad a hawful fright, I thought it were 'er as sure as measles, but look alive, Jackey. I'll go down to Bunter Street an' wait for yer, yer understand, Jackey ? "

" Aye," was the brief but sufficient answer. And without further words being wasted, Billy hurried quickly down the steps, and then more slowly down the court. His new clothes were a perfect disguise, so that he was able to leave the court as he had entered it, without recognition.

At the bottom he waited for Jack, and soon espied the little fellow toddling down the street. It was a critical moment, and Billy's heart almost stood still, so fearful was he that Mrs. Chase might come upon the scene.

Eagerly he looked up and down the street as Jack drew near, but the woman he dreaded was nowhere visible, and catching up the child in his arms he hurried away and was soon lost in the crowd.

He never paused but once—and that only for a moment to post his letter—until he reached the landing stage. Here, however, there was some considerable delay, before the railway boat started —for the new railway station at Birkenhead had

not been built then, and the Mersey Tunnel
scarcely thought of.

The boat, however, was at her berth, so Billy
and his charge went on board at once, and sought
a quiet corner in the stuffy little saloon.

" Now, Jackey," said Billy, " if ye would like to
go back to yer mother again, say so, afore it be too
late."

" Oh, no ! " answered the little fellow ; " I'd rather
go to Cricket."

" But yer can't go to her jist yet," said Billy,
huskily ; " ye shall, bymby, if ye're good."

" Then where's we going now ? " Jack asked.

" To a place called Kev-ven Lee," said Billy,
" that is, if ever we be able to find it. Yer grand-
parents live there. Did yer ever 'ear Cricket
speak on it ? "

" Oh, aye, lots of times ! " was the answer.
" Cricket often told me she'd take me there some
day."

" Well, I'm doing it instead. Now the boat's
startin' ye're sartin ye're willing to go ? "

" Aye," the little fellow answered with a smile,
and with that smile Billy's last misgivings vanished.

Perhaps it was as well he did not realise the difficulties of the undertaking, or he would scarcely
have undertaken it.

Fortunately he had just sufficient money to take
him to the nearest station to Cefn Lee, but that
was twelve miles distant, and the road that lay
between was rough and lonely in the extreme.

At Chester, he had to wait a long time for the
local stopping train, so that by the time they
reached Pontnewidd station the afternoon was
rapidly waning, and hunger was pinching both
very severely.

With his last penny he was able to get for Jack a
fairly substantial meal, and after making all neces-
sary inquiries, he started with his charge on their
long and lonely tramp to Cefn Lee.

Billy had never been in the country before, so
that he was utterly surprised and almost overcome
with fear, when, after he had left the little village
of Pontnewidd behind him, he saw stretching away
in all directions lonely reaches of mountainous
country without a single house anywhere in sight.

The road, too, was a very different affair, to the
well-paved streets he had left behind. Footpath

there was none. It seemed to him but a cart-track winding round the sides of the mountains, and leading nobody could tell whither.

Jack was too little, too tired, and too sleepy to do much walking, and too heavy to be carried without continual halts for rest. Moreover, Billy had tasted no food since morning, and so was almost ready to faint with hunger ; so that they made very slow progress along the lonely way, and Billy was beginning to despair of ever reaching their destination at all.

For the sake of Jack, however, he kept up his courage as well as he could, and betrayed no symptom of **fear or** misgiving, though he found it a very difficult matter, especially when the daylight began to fade over the tops of the mountains, and the twilight to hide the distant windings of the road.

Since they left Pontnewidd no single individual had passed them in either direction, and not a solitary footfall had broken the silence that was becoming more and more oppressive.

One thought, and one only, inspired Billy to keep pressing on, and that was, he was doing all this for Cricket's sake. She had given her life for him, and he felt that he could not do other than carry out her last wish, and take Jack to the shelter she had so often longed for him. It was true, that it seemed now as if he would fail in this. But if he failed it was not for want of trying. He had done his best. That reflection he had at least to comfort him. And what if they both died out there on the lonely mountain side? Who would care, or who would trouble? For himself he had nobody in the world to grieve for him now that Cricket was gone. Levi and Miss Bute might wonder what had become of him, but they would scarcely fret. And what was true in his case was almost, if not altogether, true in Jack's. To Cricket he was all the world, but she was gone now, and who else had he to love him, or care for him? Mrs. Chase took to him at first, as a girl takes to a new doll, but she had tired of him long since. She was not his mother, and could not have for him a mother's affection. Indeed he had little doubt but she would be heartily glad to be rid of him. While, as for the child's father, he had become so soddened and brutalised by drink as to be incapable of affection for either wife or child, and the only thing that touched his imbruted nature was that same drink that had robbed his life of all that was worth possessing, and had degraded him to a lower level than that of the beasts of the field.

What did it matter, then? If they died they would be better off, for they would go to that far-off country where Cricket was waiting for their coming, and hunger, and weariness, and cold they would know no more for ever.

"Billy," said Jack at length, "are we nearly there?"

"I reckon we be," Billy answered. "I shouldn't be surprised if we didn't see Cricket afore mornin'."

"Oh, that'll be jolly," he answered, "but it's getting very dark, an' I don't see no houses."

"Oh, don't yer mind that," said Billy, "but keep yer arms tight round my neck. I'll carry yer as far as I can, and then we'll rest. Very likely Cricket will come and fetch us afore the mornin'."

"Oh, I shall be so glad!" the little fellow answered, and then relapsed into silence.

Still Billy struggled on, hoping almost against hope that some turn in the road would reveal a human dwelling-place, where food and shelter might be found. But the darkness steadily deepened, and still no welcome lights gleamed out athwart the lonely way, and still the silence was unbroken save for the moaning of the wind, and the ripple of a stream in the valley below.

At length he gave up altogether. It was of no use trying to go any further. He was dead beat, to use his own words, and he thought he might as well die here as anywhere else.

A stunted holly bush overhanging a mossy bank seemed to offer rest and shelter.

"Are ye tired, Jackey?" he said to his companion.

"No, not very," was the answer; "but I'se very sleepy. Are we nearly there, Billy?"

"Aye, we're nearly there," said Billy, with a choking voice. "We've jist to rest 'ere a bit till Cricket comes to fetch us."

"But will she find us in the dark ?" questioned Jack.

"Oh, aye, she'll bring a light with 'er, an' she'll know where we're waitin' for 'er," Billy answered, and then seated himself on the bank, with Jack upon his knee.

"Ye're quite sure, Billy, that Cricket won't miss us ?" Jack questioned in sleepy tones.

"Quite sure, Jackey," was the reassuring answer. And then the little fellow fell asleep with his head on Billy's bosom.

Billy still tried his best to keep back the tears, but could not succeed ; his pent-up grief broke through with a rush, and for the best part of an hour he sobbed as though his heart would break. But no one saw his tears or heard his sighs save God.

There, under the shadow of the holly tree, he watched and waited for Cricket's coming. It was very lonely, and very solemn. Up the heathery mountain side the night wind swept and moaned, making sad dreamy music ; while from the valley below rose the low murmur of falling water, as it sped on its way to the distant sea. No other sounds than these broke the stillness ; no footfall was heard on the lonely way ; no message came from the far-off sky.

So Billy watched and waited for Cricket's coming, and wondered why she stayed so long.

CHAPTER XVI.

" AND YET HE WAS NOT CONTENT."

" I saw the little boy, in thought how oft that he
Did wishe of God, to 'scape the rod, a tall young man to be.
The young man rake that feles his bones with paines opprest,
How he would be a riche olde man, to live and lye at rest ;
The riche olde man that sees his end draw on so sore,
How he would be a boy againe to live so much the more."

SURREY.

HERE was some little anxiety and alarm
in Cooper's Row, when it was discovered
that little Jack Chase had mysteriously
disappeared, leaving no trace behind him.
Of course the court was searched from end
to end, and inquiries were instituted all up and down
Bunter Street, and even into Scotland Road.   Mrs.
Chase appeared to be in considerable trouble, and
vowed with tears in her eyes that if ever she got
hold of him again she would give him "sich a
warming as he'd never forget to the day of his death."

By the last delivery, however, the postman brought Billy's letter, which quickly put an end to all the excitement.

" The young fool 'll soon get tired of the brat," was Richard Chase's comment, " and ull be glad to fetch 'im back agin to-morrow."

In this view of the case his wife readily concurred, and as neither of them imagined for a moment that any harm would befall the child, while in Billy's care, they were quite content, and indeed, rather relieved than otherwise, to have him off their hands for a few hours.

As the days passed away, however, and neither Billy nor Jack returned, they began to feel curious, to say the least, as to what could have become of them.

By the end of a week, however, a letter was received from Cefn Lee, announcing that Jack had turned up in that remote region, and offering to restore him, if Richard Chase would come over and fetch him ; otherwise, he would be kept at Cefn Lee.

Richard Chase laughed immoderately on receipt of this letter. " They mun tak' me to be a downy

cove," he chuckled. "If the brat's there, let him
stay. He couldn't be in a better shop, an' they can
as well afford to keep 'im as I can, 'an a sight
better. Fetch 'im, eh ? Ha, ha. Not for Dick if
he knows it ! "

So it came about that little Jack remained at
Cefn Lee, an arrangement that seemed to be agree-
able to all concerned.

How Billy and his charge were rescued by a belated and somewhat befuddled farmer need not be
told at length. At first neither Jonas nor Martha
Evans was disposed to listen to Billy's story, or to
give the wanderers food or shelter. To be aroused
out of their first nap somewhere about the hour of
midnight in order to admit two strange children
had not tended to sweeten their tempers in the
least. But the sight of little Jack's bonny face and
large pleading eyes touched the grandmotherly
heart of Mrs. Evans in a moment, and won an easy
victory.

" I do believe it's Martha's boy after all," she said
in quaint English, for the Welsh language came much
more readily to her lips than this alien English tongue.

Even Jonas admitted that the lad was very much

like their dead daughter Martha, and when Billy was questioned relative to the matter his story was found to be so straightforward and circumstantial that there was no gainsaying it. And then to complete the chain of evidence, the shawl in which Jack was wrapped was recognised by Mrs. Evans as one she had given her daughter among several other wedding presents.

"It's real Welsh flannel this, Jonas," she said to her husband, "an' none of your English shoddy. It will last years longer yet with care, it is that tough."

So little Jack was taken to the grandmother's heart and kissed over and over again. Billy did not fare quite so well. He had no claim either upon their gratitude or hospitality.

Though satisfied that Jack was their own daughter's child, they were anything but pleased at having him thrust upon their care and protection. What could two old people do with a child of scarcely two years? Hence Billy's action was regarded with anything but favour. Indeed he was told that he had done very wickedly in thus kidnapping the child and taking him away without the consent of his parents.

Billy listened to all they had to say in almost absolute silence, only one word of defence did he offer. " It were Cricket's wish," he said, and hid his face in his hands and burst into tears.

This somewhat mollified the old people, and Molly the servant was hastily summoned down stairs to prepare a supper for the children, while Mrs. Evans proceeded to get a bed ready for their reception.

Billy stayed a week at Cefn Lee, and then through the influence of Jonas Evans, he got a situation on a farm about two miles away. For many things Billy would have preferred to have returned to Liverpool, but that would scarcely have been consistent with his promise to Cricket, " to keep his eye on little Jack."

So he took up his new life, if I may so speak, with a brave heart, and resolved, for Cricket's sake, that he would keep near her little brother.

Before a week was out, both felt the benefit of the change. The sweet fresh air of the mountains was like new life to them, after the foul air of Liverpool courts and cellars. They had come too

as Molly said, in the bonniest time of all the year,
the sweet spring time.   Already the fields were
abloom with daisies, and, in the sheltered and
sunny hedgerows, the yellow primroses were beginning to peep forth from their hiding places, while
the woods and plantations were vocal in the quiet
eventide with the songs of happy birds.   Cefn Lee
was a quaint lovable old place.   The farmhouse
was low, long and rambling, with stackyard and
" outhouses," at the back, an orchard at one end,
and a large kitchen-garden at the other, with a
smaller garden in front, which was set apart for
flowers.   The farm itself was but a small one, and
at best was a hungry stony affair.   Jonas Evans,
however, had always been a careful, diligent man,
and his wife was a worthy help-meet, and so
between them they had always made it pay, and
some years had even saved a few pounds and laid
them by against a rainy day.

They had never had but two children, Robert
and Martha.   Robert was still living and rented a
farm adjoining his father's, and so was able to give
the old man a lift in busy times.   Martha's marriage
had been a grief to all the family, though they tried

to make the best of it, and as she herself never complained, they tried to think that she was content with the lot she had chosen. So the current of their uneventful life had flowed quietly on, till news had come of Martha's death ; and now a new excitement had come in the shape of Martha's child, little Jack.

Before a month was over Jackey had established himself as a general favourite. Molly, the servant almost idolised him, and even Jonas was sometimes seen walking out across the fields, with a smile upon his wrinkled, weather-beaten face, and his grandson upon his back.

Fresh air, fresh eggs, new milk, and wholesome bread soon produced a wonderful change in the little fellow. Molly declared that if you looked at him steadily you could actually see him growing ; anyhow, in less than a year he had doubled his size and weight, and was the autocrat of the household. Neither was the change scarcely less beneficial in Billy's case. Regular meals of wholesome food, and a good bed to lie on, were luxuries that he had never known before. And though the toilsome work of the fields was not always congenial to his

nature, he knew that it was good discipline, and
therefore tried to be content.

And yet he was *not* content. The life was too
slow and prosy. It was eating, sleeping, and
working from week to week, and month to month,
with no break or change of any kind, except the
weekly Sabbath ; and even on that day cows had
to be milked, pigs fed, sheep looked up and
counted, and horses and cattle attended to. So
that before he had got half through the second
winter he had resolved to return to Liverpool again
when spring-time came, and seek his fortune in
that great city once more.

Most of my readers will think it a foolish resolve ; perhaps it was. But it is not my business
to speculate, but simply to tell the story.

Little Jack no longer needed his care or over-
sight. While as for himself, he felt that he had
learnt all that Cefn Lee and neighbourhood had
to teach him. He had been a diligent student
since he came, and had devoured all the books he
could lay hands on. He had also learned to write
fairly well, and was not altogether deficient in
arithmetic. In fact, he had learnt so much that

he was eager to learn more, but saw no chance of appeasing his hunger for knowledge while he re mained where he was. But in Liverpool—what with free lectures, free reading-rooms, free libraries, ragged-schools, Sunday-schools, night-schools, and science classes, every chance was given to those who were willing to learn. True he had spent the greater part of his life in Liverpool and had never derived any advantage from these things ; but that was because he did not know their worth. Since then he had learnt much, and in Liverpool he saw the chance of learning more.

Perhaps he would fail, perhaps he would be un-able to get work. He knew the difficulties a big city presented to a friendless lad. Still, he was not a raw country lout. Liverpool sharpers would not be able to take him in. And if he failed to get work, he would foot his way back into Wales again, and try to be content with a farm-labourer's lot.

Yet something within him told him that he would not fail. Since that memorable day, nearly two years ago, when the hospital attendant had told him that Cricket was dead, his faith in Providence had never wavered. Day by day he had tried more and more implicitly to commit his way into the hands of God, and he had no doubt that God was directing and would direct his path. He did not come to his resolution without much thought and prayer, and now that his resolve was taken nothing could turn him back.

So he went steadily on with his work till sunny April came, and then, with all his savings in his pocket, he turned his face once more towards Liverpool.

" I'll come an' see you again sometime, Jackey," he said, in answer to the little fellow's pleading look when he went to say good-bye.

" Come soon, Billy," the little fellow answered ; " and tell Cricket I do want to see her ever so bad."

" All right, Jackey," he answered, for he knew the little fellow steadily refused to believe in Cricket's death. " If I see her I'll tell her," and with a hurried kiss he was gone.

CHAPTER XVII,

"THE EXPLANATION WAS A VERY SIMPLE AFFAIR."

> " Thy voice is on the rolling air ;
> I hear thee where the waters run ;
> Thou standest in the rising sun,
> And in the setting thou art fair."
>
> TENNYSON.

TWO months passed away, when an event transpired that startled Cefn Lee from centre to circumference. It was a bright June day. All the valley was steeped in golden sunshine, and every hedge-row, and every garden was a-bloom with flowers. No sound broke the stillness, save the hum of busy bees among the garden flowers, or the occasional bleating of sheep far away up the hill sides. The watch-dogs were asleep ; the cattle lazily chewed their cuds down by the water-side in the shadow of the trees, and all nature seemed at rest.

Little Jack had been playing in the front garden, but overcome by the heat he had nearly fallen asleep, when he was startled by a footfall close to his side, and almost before he had time to look up, he was caught in somebody's arms and almost smothered with kisses, while tears like rain fell upon his cheek. For a moment he struggled to be free, much wondering what had come to him. Then a voice, choking with emotion, but which was sweeter to him than all the music of earth, spoke close to his ear.

"Oh, my little Jack, and have I found you at last?" He did not need to look up at the stranger's face. He knew the voice, and would have known it among a thousand. For two long years it had haunted his childish dreams, and filled his little life with music and with hope. And throwing his arms round the stranger's neck, he pressed his cheek close to hers.

"Oh, Cricket," he said, "I'm so glad; but I know'd you'd come."

" Did you, my darling ? " she asked, kissing him again and again.

" They said you was dead," he went on, " but I know'd you wasn't, an' I've been lookin' out for you every day."

" My darling," was all she could answer.

" But you've been very long, Cricket," he said. " But I told Billy when he went away to tell you to make haste."

" Has Billy been here ? " she asked.

" Aye, he brought me here," Jack answered quickly, " and he came every Sunday to see me ; but he's gone away again now."

" Gone away ! where ? " Cricket asked.

" Gone back to Liverpool," said Jack. " But haven't you seen him, Cricket ? "

" No, my darling, I've never seen him since he came to see me in the hospital."

" But he's a good one, is Billy," said Jack impulsively.

" I know he is " said Cricket. " I am so sorry he's gone away."

" But he'll be back again some day ; he said he would," said Jack.

And then Mrs. Evans came upon the scene, much wondering who the stranger could be.

"Oh, granny, this is Cricket," said Jack, delightedly. "I always said she'd come back."

"Nay, nay, child," said Mrs. Evans, looking much shocked. "Don't say that, Jackey."

"But I tell you, granny, it is," said Jack, stoutly. "Think I don't know Cricket."

"Well, you ought to know her," said the old woman. "But you're mistook this time, Jackey."

"Nay, grandmother, he's not mistaken," said Cricket. And then Cricket had to tell all her story, which we will summarise in as few words as possible.

The explanation, when it was given, was a very simple affair. When Billy went to the hospital to inquire after Cricket, it never seemed to have entered his head that there might be other girls in the hospital besides the one he was so anxious about. And so when the attendant asked if Cricket was the little girl that had been brought in so badly hurt, he answered readily enough, "Aye, that's her," when, as a matter of fact, it was not her at all. The little girl the attendant referred to was much younger than Cricket, and had fallen out of a third-storey window. But Billy, being so full of Cricket, had no room in his thoughts for any other little girl, and so he went away, as we have seen, never doubting for a moment that Cricket was dead.

For a full week Cricket's life trembled in the balance, and then she began gradually to recover.

In the meanwhile there had been taken into the hospital an elderly gentleman of the name of Roberts, who had broken his leg through slipping on a piece of orange-peel. During Mrs. Roberts' third visit to her husband she fell in with Cricket, and was " so taken with the girl," as she expressed it, that this casual, or chance, acquaintanceship soon ripened into a friendship, which, in Cricket's case, was not without important results.

During the first fortnight of Cricket's illness her father called to see her twice, but he never came after. This did not trouble Cricket very much, for each time he came he was in drink, and shed over her drunken tears, that gave her far more pain than consolation. To her inquiries about little Jack, he hiccoughed his answer "that the brat was all right ; never better."

Nearly three months later, when Cricket was sufficiently recovered to return to Cooper's Row, she found No. 13 occupied by strangers, and learned that her father had died of *delirium tremens* nearly a month before, and that her step-mother and Jack had gone nobody knew where.

It was a terrible blow to Cricket to find herself thus orphaned and alone. On the doorstep of the old house she sat down and cried, and in her heart wondered why God had let her get better to meet a fate like this. Naturally, in her grief, her thoughts turned to the kind old lady she had so often met at the hospital. She had her address still—No. 3, Sandy Mount, Everton. To Mrs. Roberts, then, she would go, and ask her protection for a few days until she could find some means of earning her bread.

She had no difficulty in finding the house. It was scarcely more than a cottage with a small bay window, and separated from the sidewalk by the tiniest bit of garden imaginable. Kindly, Christian, frugal people were the old gentleman and his wife. For forty years they had kept a little drapery establishment in a quiet street, and having no children, they had managed to save a few pounds every year. So that now, in their old age, they were able to retire on a competence of £150 a year.

Cricket was welcomed with every expression of pleasure and delight.

"You shall stay as long as ever you have a mind to, honey," said the old lady, "and we shall be only too glad of your company."

Elderly people are proverbially fond of having young people about them, and John and Prudence Roberts were no exception to the rule. Consequently Cricket's presence was like sunshine in the home. Before she had been in the house a fortnight she was indispensable. She relieved Mrs. Roberts of more than two-thirds of the household work, and was always so ready to oblige in every possible way that she became as a daughter to them, and filled up the one gap in the old peoples' lives.

They had often talked about keeping a servant, as Mrs. Roberts was not so "spry," as she termed it, as she once was. But after Cricket came the

P

idea was given up entirely. Cricket was servant and daughter in one.

Under these circumstances, Cricket consented to remain, and even consented at last to receive wages, only it was dubbed by the title " pocket money." She did as much work as any servant would do, and so never felt herself an intruder, nor a dependent upon the bounty of her friends. She *earned* her living, and so was content ; that is, she was content as far as she personally was concerned. But every day and every night her heart was full of anxiety respecting her little brother Jack.

As the weeks and months passed away, she instituted inquiries far and wide, she even searched herself in every likely place. Scores of miles during that summer did she tramp through the scorching streets ; but all to no purpose. Her stepmother, Billy, and Jack, had all disappeared as completely as though they had all been dead and buried.

Of her stepmother she had little thought, except as a means to an end. By finding her she might, and most probably would, find Jack ; for that Jack was still in her possession she had little doubt. And her one concern was to rescue, if possible, the little fellow from the debasing influences which surrounded him. She recognised what many others have recognised since then, that there is no chance for many children, or hope, while they remain amid present surroundings, and that only by lifting them out altogether, and placing them amid new surroundings entirely, can help be rendered to them at all.

"If Jack remains with *her* he will grow up a drunkard or something worse," was a constant thought of hers.

And this may be said of thousands of poor children to-day.

They need to be rescued from their parents, for their parents are their greatest enemies. Rescued not for a few years only, and then allowed to go back, that the parents may receive all the advantage of the training their children have received, and worse still undo and destroy all the good that Christian charity has accomplished. If lasting good is to be wrought, these poor waifs must be taken out of the clutches of their parents altogether, and *kept* out, till they are able to defend themselves.

"Better Jack should die," Cricket often said to herself, "than that he should grow up under the influence of that bad woman."

So she continued her search month after month in the only ways that were possible to her, but courage and hope almost failed her when the months lengthened into years, and no trace of either of those she was in search of could be found.

One morning, however, when going down to town (for Liverpool was not then a *city*) in an omnibus, for the purpose of making some pur-chases, and without any thought of Mrs. Chase in her mind, her attention was arrested by a face in a crowd in London Road. "That's her," was the thought that rushed through her mind like a flash of lightning.

Instantly calling upon the conductor to stop, she rushed out, and across the street, regardless of cabs and carriages, and dashed into the crowd. Yes! there could be no mistake. It was Mrs. Chase, and, trembling from head to foot, she clutched her arm and gasped out, "Oh, mother, where's Jack?"

For a moment Mrs. Chase seemed utterly dumb-founded. "*You*," she exclaimed, "where'd you spring from?"

"Never mind me," she answered, resolutely. "Where is Jack?"

"How should I know where the brat is?" she exclaimed. "I've not seen 'im for more'n two years."

"Not seen him?" said Cricket aghast.

"Nay, I've not," she said, "that young varmint Billy Walton kidnapped 'im an' walked 'im hoff to some place in Wales called Kev-ven some'at."

"And has he never come back?" Cricket asked, her face brightening.

"Never, as far as I know," said the woman, "but give us a copper, lass, for I'm 'ard up."

Cricket had a solitary half-crown in her possession that did not belong to Mrs. Roberts; instantly, and without a word, she gave it to the woman.

"Thanks, lass, thou'rt a brick," was the response, and a moment later the woman had turned a corner and was lost to sight.

For the rest of that day Cricket wandered about like one in a dream, and the following morning she set off by an early train to Cefn Lee. To describe her sensations during that journey would be impossible. Her meeting with her little brother we have already seen, and now we will leave them for a few days together, while we further pursue the fortunes of Billy Walton.

CHAPTER XVIII.

"WAS IT PROVIDENCE, I WONDER?"

" God's love is there to guide ;
  And He knows best how heavenly grace will grow.
Lo ! in the sweet, still hours of eventide
  The angels come and sow."

ADA CAMBRIDGE.

ILLY had not been in Liverpool twenty-four hours ere he felt as if he had never been away at all. All that he had passed through during the last two years seemed but a dream, and he almost wondered sometimes if he had not had a longer nap than usual and dreamed it all. Liverpool was unchanged. Its life was as vigorous; its streets as crowded as ever. For a while he stood in front of Lime Street Station watching the scene. What a hubbub! what a hurrying, scurrying crowd !

Somehow the scene was not very exhilarating. Nobody noticed him. It was very evident he was not wanted. He had gone away two years before, and Liverpool had not missed him. He had come back again, but there was no pause to give him welcome. He was but a unit in the crowd, and a very small one at that. His absence was not noticed; his presence was not felt. Never in his life did he feel smaller or more insignificant than he did that day.

Neither did he ever feel in his life more lonely. For two years he had been used to mountain solitudes, to lonely glens and valleys amongst the wild Welsh hills, and sometimes, when in search of stray sheep, he had got into glens where the silence was positively oppressive (or else he had dreamt it all), but even then, he never experienced such a sense of loneliness as he did this day. A loneliness that he was never conscious of in the old days of suffering and want.

Whatever of change there was, therefore, it was evidently all in himself. Liverpool was unchanged, but not so himself. As he looked at his reflection in shop windows (what he had never been able to do all the time he had been away), he saw that he was so altered as to be scarcely recognisable by those who had known him in the old days. He was no longer a pale, thin, hollow-eyed boy ; but a strong, brown-faced, healthy-looking lad. Pure air, pure water, pure milk, pure food, and plenty of exercise in wind and sunshine had worked wonders.

"Jabbers!" he said to himself, after contemplating his reflection for some time, "I shall be a man in no time if I go on at this rate," and away he started at a swinging pace, still on the look-out for something to do.

For the first week he was able to get hold of nothing definite or permanent. A few odd coppers he earned now and then, in carrying bags and running errands. It was while waiting in one of the Liverpool railway stations for something in this line to turn up, that the thought struck him :

"If I could get a job selling papers and books in the station, wouldn't it be glorious ?" And the more he turned this thought over in his mind, the more inviting it grew. His old passion for books was as strong as ever. To have plenty of time for reading, and plenty of books to read, was the highest ambition of his life.

"It ain't no use thinking it over," he said to himself at length ; " I'll get it settled right away," and he marched up to the book-stall, and inquired of the gentleman who stood behind if he wanted a lad to sell papers ?

"Well, yes I do," he answered slowly, after staring at Billy for several seconds. "Would you like to try your hand at it ?"

"I should, amazingly," said Billy. "I don't think there's anything I should like better."

"You could give me references as to your character, I suppose ?" the gentleman inquired.

Billy's face fell at that. Indeed he was not quite certain what "references as to character" meant.

"I mean," said the gentleman, "that you could refer me to someone who would vouch for your honesty ?"

"Oh, yes," said Billy, his face brightening ; "I've been living with Mr. Pugh, in Wales, for more'n two years ; you could write to him."

" Very good, I will write to him at once, if you will give me his correct address, and the day after to-morrow, or the day after that, you can call again, and if the reply is satisfactory I will take you on."

" I ain't afraid it won't be satisfactory," said Billy, with a grin ; and he marched away feeling as elated as if he had made a fortune.

" Now, I wonder," he said to himself, " what put that thought into my noddle ?   Was it Providence I wonder, or was it an accident ? " and for some time Billy pondered over the problem, heedless of the roar of traffic all about him, and at length arrived at the conclusion that God was watching over him still, and was guiding his steps into the right path.

" Aye, Cricket was right," he said to himself half aloud, " and religion is being good." And with this reflection he started off in the direction of Cooper's Row.

" They'll not know me," he said, " and I may be able to learn a few things." True enough nobody knew him in Cooper's Row, for every house had changed its tenants, some of them many times during the past two years. The people who occupy the courts and alleys of our large cities are not much given to settling down in one place. The home instinct, if ever they possessed it, has nearly died out, one place is as good as another, and a change is nearly always welcome.

So Billy learned nothing in Cooper's Row. Yet the sight of the old place awoke memories that had lain dormant for many a day. It was here that he had formed the truest friendship of his life. Here he had spent some of his happiest hours. Here he had first heard from the lips of Cricket those truths that were now the hope as well as the inspiration of his life. And here he had first resolved that he would try to live an honest life.

It was with a heavy sigh he turned away. "Ah, well!" he said to himself, "Cricket didn't live in vain, nor die for nothing."

During the rest of the evening, until dark, he was engaged in a diligent search for his old friend Levi Lobb, a search, however, that ended in failure, one thing only he could learn, viz., that through failing health, Levi had been obliged to give

up his situation as sexton of St. Chad's church,
and to remove to some other neighbourhood.
But to *what* neighbourhood nobody could inform
him.

When the daylight had all faded out of the sky
he took a stroll round the gloomy old church, and
looked up again at the tall spire that shot far into
the sky, and listened again to the clang of the
heavy bell as the hour of ten was boomed out
above the house tops and floated away through
the starlit night.

How memories of the past came back to him
as he loitered round ! filling him with a vague
unrest, and awaking longings within him for some·
thing which he could not define.

Back again into Cooper's Row he sauntered a
little while before the clock struck eleven.   There
was no light at No. 13, and so he sat himself on the
doorstep, and on the very spot where he had spent
that last night with Cricket two years and a half
ago.   Above him, in the narrow strip of sky, the
stars were shining as they shone that bitter night ;
and around him, as though it had never ceased,
was the roar of the city's traffic.

He had great difficulty in keeping back the tears, so vividly came back the memory of that fatal night.

" It was here she gave her life for me," he said to himself with a sigh ; " and I wonder if she knows it was not in vain. That made all she had ever told me clear, and if ever I get to heaven, I shall look out for her first thing, and tell her." So he communed with himself for the best part of an hour, and almost fancied sometimes that Cricket was sitting by his side, looking, with her great wondering eyes, at the far-off stars, and talking to him of the better home that lay far away beyond those shining points of light, in a region where darkness could never come.

Three days later Billy was installed in the situation that he never had any doubt from the first that he should get, and for twelve quiet, uneventful months he worked away with a will, earning small wages, it is true, but gaining large experience in this particular line of business.

At the end of twelve months he left his situa-jion, much to the regret of his employer, and set up in business for himself. ,He secured permission to erect a table in an unused corner in a busy thoroughfare, on which he spread his bundle of "dailies" and "weeklies," adding by-and-by "monthlies," and even "quarterlies."

To say that Billy prospered, would scarcely be correct, according to some people's notion of prosperity. He did, however, by dint of great care and economy, earn sufficient to keep him, though the "keep" was of the most frugal kind.

So two more years passed away, and then Billy embarked on a new venture. He took to buying and selling second-hand books, and discovered that on the whole it paid better than selling newspapers, and, what was better still, he had now always a book to read, and he made the most of his opportunity. So another year passed away, when he made quite a stroke of fortune. He had bought a lot of old books from a dozen different places, and one day was endeavouring to sort them, and get his stock into something like order, when a gentleman, who had been looking at several old volumes, suddenly exclaimed, as he opened a dusty, vellum-bound book. "I'll give you five pounds for this."

"I dare say you will," said Billy, carelessly; for the eagerness of the gentleman's tone convinced him in a moment that here was a treasure.

Five minutes before he would have sold his whole stock for five pounds, and have considered he had made a good bargain.

"Ah," said the gentleman, "so you know the value of rare books, do you?"

"I ought to know by this time," was the answer, though he felt that he was a bit of a hypocrite in making such a reply.

Ultimately the gentleman offered fifteen guineas for the book, but Billy wouldn't sell. An idea had struck him that certain old books were valuable in proportion to their scarcity, and he was determined to find out how far this idea was correct.

That night he closed early, and went the round of the book shops, and gathered up all the catalogues he could get hold of, and spent most of the night in studying them. As he afterwards expressed it, "they were an eye-opener" to him. Here were books catalogued at a guinea that he was certain he had in his ignorance sold for a shilling. And offers made of what seemed to him fabulous prices for rare books, or rare editions of well-known books.

In the end, Billy sold his coveted volume for thirty pounds, and felt that he had made his fortune. He had only one twinge of conscience relative to the transaction, and that was that he hadn't given the man of whom he had bought it a fair price for the book. Still, he was not to blame; for he did not know of whom he had bought the book, nor had he any idea at the time of its value.

By the end of another twelve months, Billy had given up selling newspapers altogether, and had taken a little shop in a quiet street, where he devoted all his energies to the second-hand book trade, and, as he deserved, he prospered.

In this way it will be seen that more than five years had passed away, and Billy had become a man. And now he made another discovery, which gave him both pleasure and pain, and as much of one as of the other. What that discovery was must be told in another chapter.

CHAPTER XIX.

"THEY RECOUNT AGAIN THE STORY OF THE PAST."

"What a strange life it was! Oh! if the story
Of all its joys and sorrows could be known,
How would dark shadows, mingling with its glory,
Round its whole course be thrown."

BAYNES.

T was nearly closing time, and Billy was engaged in what he termed "straightening up" for the night. He had done a good stroke of business during the day, and was feeling in very good humour with himself and with the world generally. Humming to himself a plaintive little melody, which was just now very popular at the ragged school in which he was one of the chief workers, he went steadily on with his work of "straightening up," when he was interrupted by the entrance of a barefooted lad with two books in his hand.

"Ef you please, maister, wot'll you give for these ?" said the urchin, without waiting for Billy to speak.

Billy took the books—a Bible and a prayer-book —in silence, and opening the Bible at the fly-leaf, he read, with a start,

> *Levi Lolili,*
> *His Book,*
> *March 4, 1820.*

Instantly turning to the lad, he said, excitedly, "Where did you get these books ?"

"Got 'em off Levi," said the boy. "He axed me to make as much as I could on 'em, an' fetch 'im 'ome some bacca and a crust."

"Does he live far from here ?" Billy asked, impatiently.

"No, not a werry great way," was the answer.

"Then wait a moment, and I will go with you ;" and hastily putting up the shutters, and locking the door, he followed the lad, through lanes and alleys, for a full ten minutes ; then paused at the top of a short flight of steps that led down to a cellar door.

"This way, maister," said the lad, with a grin,

and he pushed open the door and entered, closely followed by Billy.

It was a wretched room, damp, dark, and dismal, with scarcely a stick of furniture in it, and not a glimmer of fire. In a rickety wooden chair sat our old friend Levi, not only reduced in circumstances, but considerably reduced in bulk also.

He looked up in surprise as Billy entered, but no look of recognition came into his eyes. It was not likely there would, for Billy had grown into a man, and a fine handsome young fellow he was, with his thickly-curling brown hair, dark, expressive eyes, and well-knit frame.

He was glad the old man did not recognise him, for he wanted to recover himself a little ere the recognition should take place. He could have sat down and wept—wept for joy at finding the old man again, and wept for grief at finding him in such poverty.

Levi was the first to speak, for Billy could not trust himself just yet.

"I'm glad to see you, sir; very glad," he said; "an' sorry I be that I haven't got a seat to offer you."

"Don't mention it," said Billy, huskily. "I've come about those books you wished to sell."

"Oh, aye," said Levi, with an effort. "I thought I might get a few coppers for 'em, to get a bit o' bacca as would last me till to-morrow. I'm removin' from 'ere to-morrow."

"Removing?" said Billy in surprise.

"Aye," said Levi, with a gulp, brushing his hand quickly across his eyes at the same time. "You see, sir, I'm got past workin', an' I'm got a bit behind wi' the rent, so I'm 'bliged to flit."

"Might I ask where you are going?" Billy said; "that is, if you do not think the question an impertinence."

"Oh, no, not at all," said Levi; "it's very kind o' you to feel that much interest in an old man, though I don't care to talk about the place I'm going to."

"Why, is it worse than this?" Billy asked.

"I reckon most folks 'ud say it were better," Levi answered, with evident effort; "but 'ere, I've had my little room and pipe alone, an' nobody to interfere with me so long as th' rent were paid; an' that I've been used to for forty year, I fear I'll take 'ard to new ways."

"But won't you have your little room where you are going?" Billy persisted.

"I guess not," he said, with a poor wintry smile, and then commenced to mop his eyes with a tattered pocket-handkerchief.

Billy could scarcely refrain from tears himself. He guessed the old man's secret and honoured him for his reticence on 'the subject. He would not obtrude his poverty, he would not ask for help, and he was too proud to own that he was being taken on the morrow to the workhouse.

"I shall be glad to give you five shillings for your books," Billy said, after an awkward pause.

"How much?" said the old man, starting up.

"Five shillings," Billy answered.

"The Lord be praised!" said the old man, dropping into his chair again; "then I'll not go to-morrow."

Then followed another awkward pause, for both seemed too overcome to speak. Billy was the first to break the silence.

"You used to be sexton of St. Chad's Church, I think?" he said.

"Aye," answered the old man, his face brightening, " I were sexton theer for fifteen year. A fine larned man were the parson, so he got permoted soon after I were took ill wi' the bronchitis. The new parson didn't know nothin' about me, an' so I lost the place."

" Could you have kept it on had you been allowed ? " Billy asked.

" Oh aye, I think so," Levi answered. " You see, sir, I'd got hold o' a sharp little customer who helped me wi' the cleanin'. For dustin' a church an' lookin' arter the fires he had no equal. But the new parson sent word he'd 'ave no boys about. I don't know what became of the lad, but he were a smart 'un'."

" You befriended him, I think I've heard ; for I attended St. Chad's Church once," said Billy.

" I don't know as I befriended him much," said Levi ; " but I took a fancy to the little chap, an' he arned all he got."

" That's so many years ago that you would hardly know him again, if you were to see him," said Billy.

" No, likely not," said Levi ; " and he'd 'ardly know me. I'm much slimmer now, sir, than I were then, an' my breathin' gets wus an' wus, specially since my wife died. I'm nearly done, sir."

"Oh, nonsense!" said Billy, cheerfully; "you'll live a long time yet, and smoke endless pipes of tobacco."

But the old man only shook his head, while the tears filled his eyes and rolled silently down his sunken cheeks.

"You don't know me, I think," Billy said, after another pause.

"No, I've never seen you afore," said Levi; 'but you're very good, sir, to come to see an old man."

"Ah, Levi," said Billy, putting his hand on the old man's shoulder. "You've seen me many times before. I'm Billy Walton, the lad you befriended so in his greatest need."

"You Billy Walton?" said the old man, springing to his feet, and looking Billy straight in the face. "It cannot be."

"Yes, it is," said Billy, "the very same."

"The Lord have mercy," cried Levi, and fell on Billy's neck and burst into tears.

" He has had mercy," Billy answered, returning the old man's embrace. " And now, Levi, you will go home with me ; and you will never need fear the workhouse again, as long as I'm alive."

"What is that I hear?" said Levi; "I aint dreamin', am I ?"

"Oh no, you're quite wide awake. So cheer up. You helped me once, and now it is my turn to help you."

Levi made no further reply. His heart was too full for utterance. And half an hour later, he and Billy drove away in a cab together, and it would be hard to say which was the happier of the two. With careful nursing and good food the old man rapidly recovered his strength, and if in the old days Billy was useful to him, in dusting the church, so he became now equally useful to Billy in minding the shop.

Often in the days and weeks that followed they recounted again the story of the past, and laughed together over Levi's sudden downfall in the cellar, when Billy, to use Levi's phrase, "butted him in the wind ; " while on Sunday afternoons Levi went frequently with Billy to the ragged school, and sometimes undertook to teach a class himself. But Levi never had but one lesson. He always selected that chapter in Ecclesiastes commencing, " Cast thy bread upon the waters, for thou shalt find it after many days ; " and by way of illustration he told the story of his own kindness to Billy Walton, and how that little kindness had come home to him in blessings a thousand fold.

Billy was happier than he had ever been before in his life, though occasionally his conscience gave a little twinge when he thought of his promise to Cricket respecting little Jack. During all these years he had never visited Cefn Lee, nor even written to his little friend. " As for writing," he would say to himself, " what is the use of writing to a child that can't read, or write in return ? Besides, I intend to run over and see the little fellow whenever I can find the time."

But somehow he never could find the time. Every day in every week was always fully occupied, and so the weeks and months and years slipped away almost imperceptibly, and the visit was never paid.

Cricket visited Cefn Lee regularly twice a year

and from every visit returned quite disappointed that no news had yet been received of her old friend, Billy. Believing that he was still alive, his memory remained in her heart ever fresh and ever green ; while he, believing that she was dead, had long since ceased to think of her, except in quiet moments when his thoughts strayed back into the past. She thought of him as one who was living ; he thought of her as of one long dead. To him she was a sweet and precious memory, that would never wholly die. When he tried to picture her, it was as a saint, clad in white, walking the golden streets of heaven. And one of the chief attractions of that fair country was the thought of meeting her there.

As Christmas came on apace, Billy resolved that he would in some measure redeem his pledge, and visit Cefn Lee. The few matters that would need attention he could safely leave in Levi's hands.

So he wrote a letter to Farmer Evans, saying that if it were convenient he would come on Christmas Eve, and spend a day or two with them at Cefn Lee.

By return of post he got a reply written by Jack

himself, in round schoolboy hand, saying that they were all well and would be delighted to see him, and that he would have a hearty welcome and a pleasant surprise.

Jack did not say that Cricket had dictated the letter, and that she would be there to give him welcome. That was the surprise that was in store for him, and which Cricket herself had planned.

So, about noon on Christmas Eve, Billy started on his journey, little dreaming of what awaited him at the end.

CHAPTER XX.

"THE QUIET PASTURES OF PLEASURE AND OF PEACE."

> 'Holy strivings nerve and strengthen,
> Long endurance wins the crown,
> When the evening shadows lengthen,
> Thou shalt lay thy burden down."
>
> ANON.

THE short December day was drawing rapidly to a close when Billy Walton, hungry and cold, reached Cefn Lee. Cricket and Molly were alone in the house to receive him, the others, according to long-established custom, had gone across the way to spend Christmas Eve with "Our Robert," as the son was invariably called.

This arrangement would have been broken through but for Cricket. She wanted to see Billy alone, and enjoy unmolested his look of surprise when he discovered her identity.

"I'll explain matters to him," she said, "and do my best to entertain him till you come back."

Scarcely had the old people and Jack left the house when Billy arrived. Molly received him at the door with a start of surprise. Could this well-dressed young gentleman be Billy Walton?

"I should never a knowed you, sir," she said, dropping a curtsey.

"Am I so altered, Molly?" he said; "for I should have known you anywhere. You don't look a day older than when I left."

"Thank you," she said, looking pleased. "But come into the parlour. Master and missus and Jack are gone across to Robert's, they'll not be long away. But Miss Caroline is here, and will keep you company till they come back."

"Miss Caroline?" said Billy, in surprise.

"Oh! of course you don't know Miss Caroline Evans," said Molly, quite entering into the spirit of the joke. "She's a relation, an' is spendin' Christmas here. She's very nice, an' you'll soon get to know her." And Molly threw open the parlour door, and announced "Master William Walton."

It was now Cricket's turn to be surprised. All the day she had been trying to picture to herself what he would be like. But the reality upset all that she had fancied, and for the first few moments she was inclined to think that a joke had been played upon her. That this handsome young fellow could be the bare-footed, shock-headed, ill-fed urchin of other years seemed an impossibility.

"I'm sure you must be hungry, Mr. Walton," she said, when the first greetings were over, "so I will order tea at once;" and she left the room to execute her mission.

Meanwhile, Billy felt in a state of complete bewilderment. Who was this beautiful girl, whose presence filled the old farm-house with brightness, and whose voice was like music in his ears? Who did she remind him of? and what was this peculiar enchantment of her presence? He had never seen her before, never even heard of her, and yet she reminded him of something, he knew not what, long since vanished, and altogether forgotten. Where or when, in the old days, had he seen eyes like hers? and why was it that her voice struck a familiar chord, that he could not connect with any place or person.

He was still pondering over this perplexing problem, when Cricket re-entered the room.

"If you will come this way we will have tea," she said, and without a word he followed her into the roomy, comfortable old kitchen.

Suddenly the thought flashed across his mind, as he watched her pouring out a cup of tea—"Her eyes are like Cricket's, and her voice, too."

"You are a relative of the Evans's, I think?" he said abruptly, causing Cricket to look up with a start.

"Yes, on my mother's side," she answered, after a moment's pause.

"Do you know," he said, "I have been wondering, ever since I came into the house, who you are like?"

"And have you found out?" she said, archly.

"Yes. You are like—or rather you remind me of a granddaughter of Mr. Evans, the sister of Jack. You have heard of her, no doubt."

"You mean Cricket?" was the ready answer.

"Yes, I knew her quite well."

"Knew her?" said Billy, in a tone of surprise.

"Yes, at Brook Cottage," Cricket answered, evasively.

"Ah, she was very happy when she was there," he said, slowly; "but she had a hard time of it, poor girl, after she came to Liverpool. Do you know she gave her life for me?"

"No, I did not know," Cricket answered, in some confusion.

"We were alone together," he went on, "for her stepmother had locked the door against her, and so we spent the night on the doorstep; for I had no place to go any more than she had. The night was very cold, and I was very poorly clad, and so she insisted that I should have her shawl. It was very good of her, but it cost her her life."

"Indeed," said Cricket, quietly; for the conversation had taken a turn that she had not expected.

"It was good for me she came to Liverpool," he continued; "for, as I look back now upon the past, it seems to me that I owe to her everything that I possess. I should have grown up a thief but for her. She helped me when I had not a friend in the world; urged me to be honest, and encouraged me when I tried, and so her memory is the most precious thing I have, connected with the past."

Cricket did not reply to this for a moment, and then, in order to turn the conversation, she said, "It was you who brought little Jack here, I think. He will be delighted to see you."

"And I shall be delighted to see him, if only for Cricket's sake," Billy replied. "She dreaded his growing up in such an atmosphere as that of Cooper's Row, and I told her the last time I saw her that I would do my best for him."

"It was very good of you," Cricket said, with a little shake in her voice.

"Oh, no, it was nothing in comparison to what she had done for me," he replied ; "I wish I could do more, to show my respect for her memory."

Then silence fell between them till tea was over, when they repaired to the parlour once more. Cricket was pale and trembling with excitement, while Billy's thoughts were all of the past, and all his talk about the struggles of other days, in which Cricket played such an important part.

"Do you know," he said, after a long pause, "that you so remind me of Cricket that I can think of nothing else."

"I can quite account for that," she answered, quietly.

"In what way?" he asked in some surprise.

"Cannot you guess?" she said, the tears springing into her eyes. "Am I so changed that you do not know me?"

"I do not understand you," he said, looking bewildered. "What do you mean?"

"I mean that I am Cricket," she said; "you surely know me, Billy, you cannot have forgotten me quite?"

"But Cricket is dead!" he said, turning pale, and looking as startled as though he saw a ghost.

"No, no!" she said; "I did not die! It was all a mistake."

Then he got up and took her hands in his, and looked her steadily in the face.

"And you are really Cricket?" he said, his voice broken with emotion. "Yes, yes, I need not ask. How strange that our first meeting should have been on a Christmas Eve, and now, after all these years, we should meet on Christmas Eve again.

*   *   *   *   *   *

Billy remained two days longer at Cefn Lee than he had intended, and when he returned to Liverpool, it was with a heart bounding with joy and gratitude.

"It has been the happiest Christmas, Levi," he said, "that I have ever known in my life ; " and when the old man had heard his story, he remarked sententiously that he "didn't wonder." Neither did he wonder that, in the weeks and months that followed, Billy found innumerable excuses for visiting the Roberts's at No. 3, Sandy Mount.

"Anybody with half a heye can see what it's coming to," he would chuckle to himself, as he pulled steadily at his long pipe. " An' things 'ud be altogether wrong ef it didn't come to it."

*   *   *   *   *   *

Over years that followed—we need not say how many—we will draw a veil. Mr. and Mrs. Roberts, Jonas and Martha Evans, and Levi Lobb, have all gone to rest. Jack Chase farms Cefn Lee in the place of his grandfather, and a capital farmer he makes. On the spot where Brook Cottage once

stood, a modern roomy, well-appointed house now
stands, and in its pleasant rooms Cricket reigns
the queen. The hawthorn is still allowed to grow
before the door, and round its gnarled and knotted
trunk the rustic bench remains. Here, on summer
afternoons, Cricket sits and sews, and dreams.
Lifting her eyes occasionally to the far-off mountains, as the shadows deepen on their slopes, while
memories of the past crowd in upon her brain.
It seems but as yesterday since her mother sat on
the self-same spot, until she begins to recount the
experience of all the years that have rolled between,
and then the past seems to roll back and back, as
though an age had come and gone.

Is she happy? Yes, if mortals can be happy
here on earth. Look at her beautiful face, as it
catches the light of the westering sun. Look at
her wonderous eyes, so full of deep content. In
her ears is the hum of happy insects, and the
gentle ripple of the stream singing its happy song
as it used to do in the olden days ; while through
the open window floats the laughter of joyous
children filling all her heart with peace.

And now another sound greets her ear, the click

of the garden gate, and a quick, firm footstep on the gravelled path. She knows the footstep well, and turns her happy face to greet the comer.

" Why, Will, you are early to-night," she says.

" Aye, Cricket, who would stay in the smoky city if he could get away to a scene like this ? "

" Not Will Walton," she says, with a laugh. And, taking his arm, they walk away together down the garden path.

There, in the sunshine, we will leave them. They have fought their battle bravely, and now have come into the quiet pastures of pleasure and of peace.

THE END.